A SMALL PINCH

Joan Aiken was born in Rye, Sussex, and went to boarding school in Oxford. After school, she took a menial job in the BBC, then transferred to the United Nations London Information Centre. She married the UN Press Officer, Ron Brown, and left her job in 1949 to have two children. Ron died in 1955, so she returned to an editorial job on *Argosy* magazine and later transferred to advertising copywriting.

In 1961 she finished a book which she had started seven years earlier and put aside when Ron became ill. It had been called *Bonnie Green*, but the publishers suggested a more exciting title, *The Wolves of Willoughby Chase*. It came out in 1962 and did very well, due to a magnificent review in *Time* magazine. Thanks to this, Joan was able to leave full-time office work and devote herself to writing, though she still did editing and reviewing jobs at home.

Since then, for the last thirty years, she has rung the changes on novels for children, novels for adults, and collections of short stories – some for early readers, some for mid-age readers, and some for ghost-fanciers. In all she has now written about a hundred books. Joan received the MBE in 1999.

For my Mother and Martin,
and for their great-grand-descendants
Jamis and Jesse

Collins Modern Classics

A Small Pinch of Weather

and other stories

by

Joan Aiken

Illustrated by
Matilda Harrison

Collins

An Imprint of HarperCollins*Publishers*

First published by Jonathan Cape & Co. Ltd 1969
First published as a Collins Modern Classic 2000

3 5 7 9 10 8 6 4

Collins Modern Classics is an imprint of HarperCollins*Publishers* Ltd,
77-85 Fulham Palace Road, Hammersmith, London W6 8JB

The HarperCollins website address is
www.**fire**and**water**.com

Copyright © Joan Aiken 1969
Postscript copyright © Joan Aiken 2000
Illustrations copyright © Matilda Harrison 2000

The author and illustrator assert the moral right
to be identified as the author and illustrator of this work.

ISBN 0 00 675489-9

Printed and bound in Great Britain by
Omnia Books Limited
Glasgow, G64

CONTENTS

One

A SMALL PINCH OF WEATHER

PETRONILLA'S GUEST HOUSE, where the Bishop stayed, was next door to a little shop with small unimpressive windows containing a mixed-up tangle of things which nobody ever looked at, because they always walked straight into the shop and told Miss Sophy Ross what they wanted, and she always had it, whether it was three ounces of three-ply for a jersey or half a mile of mare's-tail for Tuesday.

The previous woolmonger before Miss Sophy had been an old lady who had called the shop 'Joy'. The signboard read like this:

Wools and **JOY** Embroidery

with the JOY in bigger letters to show it was intended to be read first. Of course nobody ever did. They called the shop 'Wools and Joy'. When the old lady died Sophy's father gave her the shop for a twenty-first birthday present and suggested she should change the name to 'Wools and Sophy', but she preferred to call it 'Wools and WEATHER Embroidery', and had the sign changed accordingly.

The town of Strathcloud, where the Ross family lived, still employed an official Weather Witch. The post was hereditary. So at twenty-one Sophy had automatically become Weather Operator for the Strathcloud Urban District Council at a salary of four pounds a year, a bushel of sunflower seeds, and free upkeep of her bicycle.

Her duties were simple: she had to provide suitable weather for any town occasion, such as Bonfire Night or the ceremonial ducking of the Provost which took place on April 1st. And when these fixtures were dealt with she was free to make weather bookings for any private citizens who wanted them, provided they did not conflict.

"Half an hour's rain for your carrots, Mr McCrae, Tuesday morning? I'm afraid eleven thirty to twelve is booked sunny for Mrs Lowrie – Janet Lowrie's wedding, you know; would twelve to twelve thirty suit? Fine rain, or medium fine? And do you want any wind with it?"

There was no charge for the weather itself, but a sixpenny booking fee which went towards municipal expenses.

When the Bishop of Mbutambuta retired from Africa and came to live in Strathcloud he stayed at Petronilla's Guest House. On his first day exploring the town he was attracted by the 'Wools and WEATHER Embroidery' notice. He wandered into the shop and stared round at the crochet hooks, dangling skeins of wool, needle measures, rain gauges, and wind-scales.

"Guid morning," said Miss Sophy, "what can I do for you?"

It was impossible to tell Miss Sophy's age. She had not changed since she took office at twenty-one. She was small, her face was nut-shaped and nut-brown, her hair was mousy, and her eyes were grey. There was something a little vague and misty about her but she had a nice smile.

"Oh, I'd like a hem-stitched sunset, please," said the Bishop absently, looking at Miss Sophy, "and half a pound of three-ply hail."

The Bishop and Miss Sophy became good friends for a short time. The Bishop had been acquainted with rain-making witch-doctors in Mbutambuta and was interested to find the old custom kept up in Scotland.

"Where does your weather end?" he asked. "Does it extend to Farquhidder?"

"Oh no, that would never do!" said Miss Sophy, shocked. "The weather stops at the parish boundary, of course. Sometimes in a drought we get people standing there with buckets and hoses trying to siphon off our rain."

"Why don't they make their own rain?"

"Och well, they've never had a weather witch in Farquhidder."

Miss Sophy was very fond of every kind of weather. When her duties permitted, she liked to go out in the rain or the mist of the sun, riding her bicycle over the moors and watching the clouds whirl across the sky or the raindrops slide off the end of her handlebars. The Bishop was a great walker, and sometimes she would see him, always equipped with his umbrella, striding up the local mountain or down one of its glens.

But alas, Miss Sophy had very little spare time. That was one of the penalties of the job: she had to be always within reach or near at hand in case of emergency calls on her services.

The trouble between Miss Sophy and the Bishop was due to Sophy's sunshine-coloured cat, Tomintoul.

The Bishop slept up on the top storey of Petronilla's Guest House, in a large spacious room with a picture window and a skylight.

Recently Tomintoul had taken to roaming at night. Perhaps he found Miss Sophy's diet insufficient for his large frame – she lived mostly on fried eggs, done sunny side up, Apple Snow, and Sunshine Cake with Ice-Cream Frosting. Whether Tomintoul hoped for better things at the Guest House, or whether he had personal affairs farther afield, who can say? At all events he went out several times a week, and the route he took was over the roof and through the room occupied by the Bishop, who was quite unused to having a large, dew-spangled cat descend on him heavily in the middle of the night. The first time it happened he thought Tomintoul was a python (they had been the chief nuisance in Mbutambuta) and leapt yelling across the room. The second time he didn't wake up, but as Tomintoul, finding the door shut, spread his large form across more and more of the bed, the Bishop began to suffer from strange dreams. He thought he was being hugged by bears, run over by steam-rollers, drowned in a river full of crocodiles.

Next morning found Tomintoul placidly washing in the middle of the bed while its rightful owner dangled in a fold of blanket at one side.

The Bishop felt he was being treated with lack of respect, and complained to Miss Dalziel, who ran the Guest House.

"Och, awa', could ye not keep the skylight shut?" she suggested.

"That is out of the question," said the Bishop firmly. "It was in order to benefit from the crisp, healthy air that I came to Scotland. If this persecution continues I doubt if it will be possible for me to make a prolonged stay at your otherwise delightful Guest House, where I had hoped to spend my declining days."

"Well, noo, we could find you anither room."

"But I like the outlook from this one. All that is needful is that the cat be shut in at night."

But when Miss Sophy heard this suggestion she exclaimed, "Shut in Tomintoul? Impossible! Besides, I need to study the condition of his fur in the morning. It tells me a lot about the weather."

Unfortunately Tomintoul's wanderings became more and more frequent. Next night he arrived on the Bishop at two a.m. with a large mouse, alighting so heavily that the

Bishop, who was dreaming that he was aboard the *Titanic*, shouted, "Abandon ship! Man the lifeboats!"

No Bishop likes to feel ridiculous. Next morning he determined to curse Tomintoul with bell, book and candle. As it happened, however, the ship in which he had travelled from the Gold Coast had been overrun by mice, and his stock of cursing candles had been consumed at lively mouse-parties. The Bishop entered MacGregor's Stores at nine o'clock next morning and asked for a pound of their largest candles.

"I'm afraid we're clean out of candles," said Miss Maggie MacGregor. "Can I sell you a nice wee electric torch, now?"

"Oh, leave it, leave it," the Bishop said wearily. In mitigation of his irritability it must be remembered that he was low on sleep.

Miss Sophy was dreamily stacking pink, blue and green wools into a rainbow-coloured pyramid and gazing at the weather outside (a nice drizzle, lightly touched with sleet) when the Bishop stormed in.

"This must stop!" he said accusingly.

"Only another ten minutes," said Sophy comfortably, "and then we're due for a rainbow to coincide with the children's break. Don't you like rain? Can I sell you some wool? Many retired clerical gentlemen take to knitting."

And before he knew where he was the Bishop had bought eighteen ounces of fisherman's-knit and two immense wooden needles.

He took the bus to Farquhidder to buy a catapult, and a

quantity of netting, and a potato pistol, and a fire-extinguisher.

After he had made these purchases he dropped into a café for a cup of tea, and there chanced to overhear a very odd conversation.

"Going to the races, Thursday?" a weaselly-looking little man was saying to another who was rather like a tall guinea-pig, hairless, with pink eyes.

"Why, got any good tips?"

"I've one *very* good tip." Weasel leaned closer and looked sharply about. "You remember MacPhair's Marsh Marigold? The mare that only runs well when the going's sticky?"

"I thought he'd given up running her."

"Man, he's had a stroke of genius. Ye ken Strathcloud, where they have the lass that sees to the weather?"

"He's never going to—"

"Hush, man! Listen to this!" Weasel leaned closer and the Bishop heard the words "rowan... soon settle her." He thought to himself that if Marsh Marigold's winning the race depended on someone trying to bribe Miss Sophy, then the horse's backers were out of luck. For though he would gladly have transported her and her cat to the farthest Antipodes, the Bishop was quite sure Miss Sophy would never be party to such a plan.

When Tomintoul came to call on the Bishop very early next morning he received a rude shock. Jumping down through the skylight he found himself entangled in innumerable folds of strawberry netting and the Bishop bombarded him with potato pellets and sprayed him with detergent foam. Tomintoul was affronted.

"And you can stay there till after breakfast to teach you the sanctity of the English home," the Bishop said crossly, and went down to his porridge, leaving Tomintoul in a sadly ruffled condition, sniffing the heartbreaking fragrance of kippers that wafted up the stairs.

After breakfast the Bishop went for a short stroll, according to custom. But the weather was inclement (in fact it was raining cats and dogs) and he soon turned homewards. As he neared the Guest House he noticed an anxious crowd gathered outside the wool-shop next door.

Miss Dalziel was there, and Mr McCrae, and Mrs Lowrie, and Miss Maggie MacGregor, and a great many other people, some inside the shop and some on the step, all looking worried and distressed.

"Oh, Bishop dear!" Miss Dalziel burst out as soon as he came within earshot, "you'll not have seen Miss Sophy the morn? It's not like her to leave the shop, but no one's laid eyes on her since eight o'clock!"

"No, I haven't seen her," said the Bishop. Then he remembered Tomintoul, still incarcerated upstairs. Would the cat's imprisonment have anything to do with Miss Sophy's absence? Hurriedly excusing himself he went up to his bedroom where Tomintoul, making the best of a bad job, had curled up and gone to sleep.

"Wake up," said the Bishop, "your mistress is missing." He loosed Tomintoul from the nets, and took him down to the shop. By this time the police had arrived and were searching for clues, but not finding any.

"We'll need to be telling the Provost of this," said Inspector Trootie. "But he's awa' doon at the races all day today."

The races! Only then did the Bishop remember the ominous conversation he had overheard in the café at Farquhidder. He told Inspector Trootie about it.

"Man! Then it's as plain as can be! Yon miscreants will have kidnapped her and be forcing her to make a bit of rain for them."

"Och, maircy, the puir lassie," lamented Miss Dalziel. "Whatever shall we do for weather without her? Saints presairve us, it'll never stop raining!"

But just at that moment the rain did stop in a sudden and most decisive manner. The sun came out and shone as if it intended to go on shining all night.

"Good for the lassie, she's defying the scoondrels!" exclaimed Inspector Trootie. "I wonder, noo, where they'll have taken her? We'll be needing police-dogs, to follow the scent and the mischance of it is they're all in Hyde Park, taking part in the sheep-dog trials."

"Could we no put Tomintoul on the trail?" suggested Miss Dalziel.

"Ah, it's easy to see ye've had a hand in the administrative side of things, ma'am," said Inspector Trootie admiringly.

Tomintoul had vanished again. After some searching he was discovered back in Petronilla's Guest House, availing himself of the kipper skins. He was brought back licking his whiskers and put on to the scent at the wool-shop door, though, as the Inspector observed, "If he can deduce onything through yon reek of kipper he's better than a marvel."

The weather was behaving very oddly. In a series of short spells they had a fog, sleet, snow, wind that shot up from gale Force Seven to Twelve and then back to Six, rainbows, snow-bows, blistering sun, and a very muddling series of mirages due to the constant variation in air temperature.

"I doot they're subjecting her to pressure," Inspector Trootie said unhappily.

Tomintoul was a very slow tracker. He kept sitting down to wash, and this was maddening for the pursuers.

Old McCrae said dourly, "I've heard tell of tracking doon wrong-doers with a posse, but aiblins this is the first time it's ever been pairpitrated with a pussy."

Tomintoul stuck his right hind leg over his head and looked inscrutably under it at Mr McCrae.

The Bishop couldn't bear the pace. He had been used to striding through the bush at a smart four miles an hour, and he soon decided to strike off on his own. Besides, he hadn't much faith in Tomintoul's judgment, and he had been visited by another idea. He climbed the side of Glasdeir, the local mountain, until he reached the bottom end of a lonely glen with a single rowan tree in it.

Meanwhile Tomintoul had dismayed the trackers by returning to Petronilla's Guest House and asking in an emphatic manner for more kipper skins. The Inspector thought it would be best if his request was granted, so they all stood round impatiently while he ate two or three. Then he picked up one very large skin and carried it slowly through the village.

"And what do ye suppose will be the meaning of that?" said Inspector Trootie.

"Hoots, man, can ye not see the guid-hearted cattie is taking a wee bit fush to his mistress in distress?"

"We shan't reach her till Hogmanay at this rate," the Inspector said gloomily. "Do ye suppose Tomintoul would let me carry the fush?"

But Tomintoul scorned any such suggestion, and went on sit-down strike, growling loudly every time the Inspector tried to approach him. Matters had to be left as they were. The procession wound at a snail's pace down to the bridge over the Hirple Burn and up the hill on the other side towards Mudie's Barn.

At about this time the Bishop, approaching his rowan tree along the craggy and twisting glen, heard a series of angry shouts and a faint cry for help. Nodding grimly to himself he rounded the last corner of rock and beheld a strange scene.

Four or five louts (if he had been Inspector Trootie he would have known they were the Wild Wee Lads, alias the Ardnafechtan Gang), including the weaselly man from the café, had the poor little Weather Witch tied up in the high fork of the rowan tree, where she looked most uncomfortable. Two of them carried axes, and a couple more were piling up dried bracken and whin round the bole of the tree.

"Now for the last and lucky time, lass, will you obleege us with a bit rain?" snarled Hughie Hogg, the weaselly man. "We'd hate to cause you unnecessary suffering, but it's airgently needful for oor plans that the groond should be soaked by three o'clock. If ye will not grant this reasonable request we'll be forced to chop half through the tree and set fire to it."

"I can't let you have any rain," Miss Sophy answered resolutely. "In the first place you are not Strathcloud rate-payers, and in the second this afternoon's booked fine to dry the Strathcloud Wanderers' football wash."

"Give her a taste of smoke, Donald," said Hughie. "If we warm her up enough she'll likely make a bit of rain to dowse the fire."

Donald lit a patch of furze and the smoke puffed up into poor Sophy's face. At the same moment Hughie swung his axe with an ominous clunk against the tree. But the sky remained obstinately blue and cloudless, the sun shone indefatigably.

"You'll have terrible bad luck if you chop a rowan tree," the Weather Witch said faintly. Then her head drooped sideways and she slipped down in the cords that held her. It was plain that she was unconscious.

"She'll come to soon enough when the fire burns up under her toes," said Donald callously.

"Get her down at once, you abominable blackguards!" snapped the Bishop, waving his umbrella.

The gang spun round in amazement. In their absorption they had not noticed him coming. But when they realized they had only an elderly clerical gentleman to deal with they relaxed, and began to close in on him menacingly.

"Ye'll be sorry you came up here, Daddy-O," said Hughie.

"Are you going to get that lady down or not?"

"Are you oot of your mind, man? After all the trouble we've taken to put her there?"

"Then I shall be obliged to shout," said the Bishop, putting his hands over his ears.

"Shout and be dommed to ye. There's no one nearer than Strathcloud," said Donald, who had run up and reconnoitred from the shoulder of the glen.

The Bishop's shout was a most unusual sound. It had an electrifying effect on the gang. Without a single exception they dropped to the ground as if they had been pole-axed, and lay motionless.

"Miss Sophy!" called the Bishop. "Are you all right?"

But it was plain that she was still unconscious, and unfortunately the pile of dried furze beneath her was now blazing merrily.

The Bishop took out of his pocket a neatly woven grass string, from which dangled a small cluster of bones. He addressed these in a stern, commanding voice.

"Rain, if you please. And make haste."

Grey clouds came scurrying across the sky like poultry running to be fed, and unloosed their contents in a torrential downpour directly over the spot where the Bishop stood. He hastily opened his umbrella.

In less than no time the bonfire was quenched and the bishop was able to climb the rowan and rescue Miss Sophy who was recovering under the reviving effect of a nice drop of rain.

"Oh," she sighed, "how delicious." Then rousing a little more she remembered the situation and exclaimed, "Oh, but this will never do! There was no rain scheduled for this afternoon!"

"Don't be alarmed," said the Bishop, "this storm is extremely local." He took off his hat and addressed the teeming heavens.

"You may now stop. I am extremely obliged to you."

"Good gracious," said Miss Sophy weakly, "who taught you to do that?"

"Oh, I learned it from a witch-doctor in Mbutambuta," the Bishop said modestly.

"But how did you dispose of the gang?"

"I used a battle-shout which was taught me by the same man. It is most efficacious – in fact it has a literally stunning effect. N'Doko was able to kill people with it, but luckily I am not so proficient. However those men should stay unconscious long enough for the police to get here."

He picked up Miss Sophy and carried her carefully down the glen.

Where, meanwhile, were the police?

With the rest of the townspeople of Strathcloud they were in Mudie's Barn, indignantly surveying the object of Tomintoul's pilgrimage, a lissom black mother cat and three fine kittens. Tomintoul, intensely proud at all this public notice, gave his wife the kipper skin and set about washing his children.

"The auld wretch! He desairves to be jailed for contempt – leading us a wild-goose-chase like this!" cried Miss Dalziel indignantly.

Inspector Trootie was more philosophical. "Aweel, aweel, hoo was he tae ken whit we were seeking? We'll juist have ti gae on sairching for the puir wee leddy."

"But where?" wailed Miss Maggie MacGregor.

Her question was soon answered, for they met the Bishop and Miss Sophy by the bridge.

The Bishop never told the police how he had managed to subdue the Ardnafechtan Gang, and they themselves had no theories about it. But they never tried to interfere with the Weather Witch of Strathcloud again.

From that day the Bishop and Miss Sophy were firm friends again. Tomintoul's family were brought down to the wool-shop (where they wrought terrible havoc, but nobody minded) so he had no need to go out over roof-tops at night to visit them.

In due course the black kitten went to live with the Bishop, who christened him Kattegat, and it was an interesting fact that, although Kattegat slept on the Bishop's bed, taking up more and more room as he grew larger and larger, the Bishop never again threatened to leave Petronilla's Guest House. Indeed he soon fell into the habit of giving Miss Sophy a hand with the weather, if she was ever a bit under it, or wanted a day off to go blaeberry picking.

The Bishop never achieved Sophy's lightness of touch with the elements though; and when the sun shone hot enough to fry an egg, or the wind shot up to Beaufort Scale Twelve, or the hailstones were as large as Seville oranges, the good people of Strathcloud would shake their heads and remark,

"Ah, to be sure, yon's a touch o' Bishop's Weather."

Two

BROOMSTICKS AND SARDINES

"OH, BOTHER," SAID Mrs Armitage, looking over her coffee-cup at the little heap of sixpences on the sideboard, "the children have forgotten to take their lunch money to school. You could go that way to the office and leave it, couldn't you, darling?"

The house still reverberated to the slam of the front door, but the children were out of sight, as Mr Armitage gloomily ascertained.

"I hate going to that place," he said. "Miss Croot makes me feel so small, and all the little tots look at me."

"Nonsense, dear. And anyway, why shouldn't they?" Mrs Armitage returned in a marked manner to the *Stitchwoman and Home Beautifier's Journal*, so her husband, with the sigh of a martyr, put on his hat, tucked *The Times* and his umbrella under his arm, and picked up the money.

He dropped a kiss on his wife's brow, and in his turn went out, but without slamming the door, into the October day. Instead of going down the cobbled hill towards his office he turned left up the little passageway which led to Miss Croot's kindergarten, which Mark and Harriet attended. It was a small studio building standing beside a large garden which lay behind the Armitage garden; Harriet and Mark often wished that they could go to school by climbing over the fence. Fortunately the children were not allowed to play in the studio garden or, as the Armitage parents often said to each other, shuddering, they would hear their children's voices all day long instead of only morning and evening.

Mr Armitage tapped on the studio door but nobody answered his knock. There was a dead hush inside, and he mentally took his hat off to Miss Croot for her disciplinary powers. Becoming impatient at length, however, he went in, through the lobby where the boots and raincoats lived. The inner door was closed, and when he opened it he stood still in astonishment.

The studio room was quite small, but the little pink and blue and green desks had been shoved back against the walls to make more space. The children were all sitting cross-legged on the floor, quiet as mice, in a ring round the old-fashioned green porcelain stove with its black chimney-pipe which stood on a kind of iron step in the middle of the room. There was a jam cauldron simmering on this stove, and Miss Croot, an exceedingly tall lady with teeth like fence-posts and a great many bangles, was stirring the cauldron and dropping in all sorts of odds and ends.

Mr Armitage distinctly heard her recite:

"Eye of newt and toe of frog…"

and then he said: "Ahem," and, stepping forward, gave her the little stack of warm sixpences which he had been holding in his hand all this time.

"My children forgot their lunch money," he remarked.

"Oh, thank you, Mr Er," Miss Croot gratefully if absently replied. "*How* kind. I do like to get it on Mondays. Now a pinch of vervain, Pamela, from the tin on my desk, please."

A smug little girl with a fringe brought her the pinch.

"I hope, ma'am, that *that* isn't the children's lunch," said Mr Armitage, gazing distastefully into the brew. He saw his own children looking at him pityingly from the other side of the circle, plainly hoping that he wasn't going to disgrace them.

"Oh dear, no," replied Miss Croot vaguely. "This is just our usual transformation mixture. There, it's just going to boil." She dropped in one of the sixpences, and it instantly became a pink moth and fluttered across to the window.

"Well, I must be on my way," muttered Mr Armitage. "Close in here, isn't it."

He stepped carefully back through the seated children to the doorway, noticing as he did so some very odd-looking maps on the walls, a tray of sand marked in hexagons and pentagons, a stack of miniature broomsticks, coloured beads arranged on the floor in concentric circles, and a lot of little Plasticine dolls, very realistically made.

At intervals throughout the day Mr Armitage thought rather uneasily about Miss Croot's kindergarten, and when he was drinking his sherry that evening he mentioned the matter to his wife.

"Where are the children now, by the way?" he said.

"In the garden sweeping leaves with their brooms. They made the brooms themselves, with raffia."

In fact he could see Mark and Harriet hopping about in the autumn dusk. They had become bored with sweeping and were riding on the brooms like horses. As he watched, Mark shouted "Abracadabra" and his broomstick lifted itself rather jerkily into the air, carried him a few yards, and then turned over, throwing him into the dahlias.

"Oh, jolly good," exclaimed Harriet. "Are you hurt? Watch me now." Her broomstick carried her into the fuchsia bush, where it stuck, and she had some trouble getting down.

"You see what I mean?" said Mr Armitage to his wife.

"Well, I shouldn't worry about it too much," she answered comfortably, picking up her tatting. "I think it's much better for them to get that sort of thing out of their systems when they're small. And then Miss Croot is such a near neighbour; we don't want to offend her. Just think how tiresome it was when the Bradmans lived there and kept dropping all their snails over the fence. At least the children play quietly and keep themselves amused nowadays, and that's *such* a blessing."

Next evening, however, the children were being far from quiet.

Mr Armitage, in his study, could hear raucous shouts and recriminations going on between Mark and Harriet and the Shepherd children, ancient enemies of theirs in the garden on the other side.

"Sucks to you!"

"Double sucks, with brass knobs on."

"This is a gun, I've shot you dead. Bang!"

"This is a magic wand, I've turned you into a—"

"*Will* you stop that hideous row," exclaimed Mr Armitage, bursting out of his French window. A deathly hush fell in the garden. He realized almost at once, though, that the silence was due not so much to his intervention as to the fact that where little Richard, Geoffrey and Moira Shepherd had been, there were now three sheep, which Harriet and Mark were regarding with triumphant satisfaction.

"Did you do that?" said Mr Armitage sharply to his children.

"Well – yes."

"Change them back at once."

"We don't know how."

"Geoffrey – Moira – your mother says it's bed-time." Mr Shepherd came out of his greenhouse with a pair of secateurs.

"I say, Shepherd, I'm terribly sorry – my children have changed yours into sheep. And now they say they don't know how to change them back."

"Oh, don't apologize, old chap. As a matter of fact I think it's a pretty good show. Some peace and quiet will be a wonderful change, and I shan't have to mow the lawn." He shouted indoors with the liveliest pleasure,

"I say, Minnie! Our kids have been turned into sheep, so you won't have to put them to bed. Dig out a long frock and we'll go to the Harvest Ball."

A shriek of delight greeted his words.

"All the same, it was a disgraceful thing to do," said Mr Armitage severely, escorting his children indoors. "How long will it last?"

"Oh, only till midnight – like Cinderella's coach, you know," replied Harriet carelessly.

"It would be rather fun if *we* went to the Harvest Ball," remarked Mr Armitage, in whom the sight of the carefree Shepherd parents had awakened unaccustomed longings. "Agnes could look after the children, couldn't she?"

"Yes, but I've nothing fit to wear!" exclaimed his wife. "Why didn't you think of it sooner?"

"Well, dash it all, can't the kids fix you up with something? Not that I approve of this business, in fact I'm going to put a stop to it, but in the meantime…"

Harriet and Mark were delighted to oblige and soon provided their mother with a very palatial crinoline of silver lamé.

"Doesn't look very warm," commented her husband, "remember the Assembly Rooms are always as cold as the tomb. Better wear something woolly underneath."

Mrs Armitage created a sensation at the ball, and was so sought-after that her husband hardly saw her the whole evening. All of a sudden, as he was enjoying a quiet game of whist with the McAlisters, a terrible thought struck him.

"What's the time, Charles?"

"Just on twelve, old man. Time we were toddling. I say, what's up?"

Mr Armitage had fled from the table and was frantically searching the ballroom for his wife. At last he saw her, right across on the other side.

"Mary!" he shouted. "You must come home at once."

"Why? What? Is it the children…?" She was threading her way towards him when the clock began to strike. Mr Armitage started and shut his eyes. A roar of applause broke out, and he opened them again to see his wife looking down at herself in bewilderment. She was wearing a scarlet silk ski-suit. Everyone was crowding round her, patting her on the back and saying that it was the neatest trick they'd seen since the pantomime and how had she done it? She was given a prize of a hundred cigarettes and a bridge marker.

"I had the ski-suit on underneath," she explained on the way home. "So as to keep warm, you see. There was plenty of room for it under the crinoline. And what a mercy I did…"

"All this has got to stop," pronounced Mr Armitage next morning. "It's Guy Fawkes in a couple of weeks, and can't you just imagine what it'll be like – children flying around on broomsticks and being hit by rockets, outsize fireworks made by fancy methods that I'd rather not go into – it just won't do, I tell you."

"*Je crois que vous faites une montagne d'une colline – une colline de…*"

"*Une taupinière,*" supplied Harriet kindly. "And you can call father '*tu*', you know."

Mark looked sulkily into his porridge and said, "Well, we've got to learn what Miss Croot teaches us, haven't we?"

"I shall go round and have a word with Miss Croot."

But as a result of his word with Miss Croot, from which Mr Armitage emerged red and flustered, while she remained imperturbably calm and gracious, such very large snails began to march in an endless procession over the fence from Miss Croot's garden into the Armitage rose-bed, that Mrs Armitage felt obliged to go round to the school and smooth things over.

"My husband always says a great deal more than he means, you know," she apologized.

"Not at all," replied Miss Croot affably. "As a matter of fact I am closing down at Christmas in any case, for I have had a most flattering offer to go as instructress to the young king of Siam."

"Thank goodness for *that*," remarked Mr Armitage. "I

should think she'd do well there. But it's a long time till Christmas."

"At any rate the snails have stopped coming," said his wife placidly.

Mr Armitage issued an edict to the children.

"I can't control what you do in school, of course, but understand that if there are any more of these tricks outside school there will be *no* Christmas tree, *no* Christmas party, *no* stockings, and *no* pantomime."

"Yes, we understand," said Harriet sadly.

Mrs Armitage, too, looked rather sad. She had been thinking what a help the children's gifts would be over the shopping; not perhaps with clothes, as nobody wanted a wardrobe that vanished at midnight, but food! Still, would there be very much nourishment in a joint of mutton that abandoned its eaters in the middle of the night? Probably not; it was all for the best.

Mark and Harriet faithfully, if crossly, obeyed their father's edict, and there were no further transformations in the Armitage family circle. But the ban did not, of course, apply to the little Shepherds. Richard, Geoffrey and Moira were not very intelligent children, and it had taken some time for Miss Croot's teaching to sink into them, but when it did they were naturally anxious to retaliate for having been turned into sheep. Mark and Harriet hardly ever succeeded in reaching school in their own shape; but whether they arrived as ravens, moths, spiders, frogs or pterodactyls, Miss Croot always changed them back again with sarcastic politeness. Everyone became very bored with the little Shepherds and their unchanging joke.

Guy Fawkes came and went with no serious casualties, however, except a few broken arms and legs and cases of concussion among the children of the neighbourhood, and Mrs Armitage began making plans for her Christmas Party.

"We'll let the children stay up really late this year, shall we?" she said. "You must admit they've been very good. And you'll dress up as Father Christmas, won't you?"

Her husband groaned, but said that he would.

"I've had such a bright idea. We'll have the children playing Sardines in the dark; they always love that; then you can put on your costume and sack of toys and get into the hiding-place with them, and gradually reveal who you are. Don't you think that's clever?"

Mr Armitage groaned again. He was always sceptical about his wife's good ideas, and this one seemed to him particularly open to mischance. But she looked so pleading that he finally agreed.

"I must make a list of people to ask," she went on. "The Shepherds, and the McAlisters, and their children, and Miss Croot, of course…"

"*How* I wish we'd never heard of that woman's school," said her husband crossly.

Miss Croot was delighted when Mark and Harriet gave her the invitation.

"I'll tell you what would be fun, children," she said brightly. "At the end of the evening I'll wave my wand

and change you all into dear little fairies, and you can give a performance of that Dance of the Silver Bells that you've been practising. Your parents *will* be surprised. And I shall be the Fairy Queen. I'll compose a little poem for the occasion:

"Now, dear parents, you shall see
What your girls and boys can be,
Lo, my magic wand I raise
And change them into elves and fays...

"or something along those lines."

And she retired to her desk in the throes of composition, leaving the children to get on with copying their runes on their own.

"I think she's got a cheek," whispered Mark indignantly. "After all, it's our party, not hers."

"Never mind, it won't take long," said Harriet, who was rather fond of the Dance of the Silver Bells and secretly relished the thought of herself as a fairy.

The party went with a swing; from the first game of Hunt the Slipper, the first carol, the first sight of Mrs Armitage's wonderful supper with all her specialities, the turkey *vol-au-vent* and Arabian fruit salad.

"Now how about a game of Sardines?" Mrs Armitage called out, finding with astonishment that it was half-past eleven and that none of her guests could eat another crumb.

The lights were turned out.

"Please, we'd rather not play this game. We're a bit nervous," twittered the Shepherd children, approaching their hostess. She looked at them crossly — really they *were* faddy children.

"Very well, you sit by the fire here till it's time for the Tree." As she left them she noticed that they seemed to be drawing pictures in the ashes with their fingers, messy little beasts.

She went to help her husband into his cloak and beard.

"Everyone is in the cupboard under the stairs," she said. "Harriet hid first, and I told her to go there. I should give them another minute."

"Who's that wandering about upstairs?"

"Oh, that's Miss Croot. Her bun came down, and she went up to fix it. Don't wait for her — there you are, you're done. Off with you."

Father Christmas shouldered his sack and went along to the stair cupboard.

"Well," he exclaimed, in as jovial a whisper as he could manage, stepping into the thick and dusty dark, "I bet you can't guess who's come in this time?" Gosh, I do feel a fool, he thought.

Silence greeted his words.

"Is there anybody here?" he asked in surprise, and began feeling about in the blackness.

Mrs Armitage, standing by the main switch, was disconcerted to hear shriek upon shriek coming from the cupboard. She threw on the light and her husband came reeling out, his beard awry, parcels falling from his sack in all directions.

"Fish!" he gasped. "The whole cupboard's full of great wriggling fish."

It was at this moment that Miss Croot appeared in full fig as the Fairy Queen, and began to recite:

"Now, dear parents, you shall see
What your girls and boys can be..."

A somewhat shamefaced procession of large silver fish appeared from the cupboard and began wriggling about on their tails.

"Oh dear," said Miss Croot, taken aback. "This wasn't what I—"

"D.T.s," moaned Mr Armitage. "I've got D.T.s." Then his gaze became fixed on Miss Croot in her regalia, and he roared at her:

"Did you do this, woman? Then out of my house you go, neck and crop."

"Mr Armitage!" exclaimed Miss Croot, drawing herself up, stiff with rage, and she would certainly have turned him into a toad, had not an interruption come from the little Shepherds, who danced round them in a ring, chanting:

"Tee hee, it was us, it was us! Sucks to the Armitages!"

Luckily at that moment the clock struck twelve, the fish changed back into human form, and by a rapid circulation of fruit-cup, cherry ciderette, and the rescued parcels, Mrs Armitage was able to avert disaster.

"Well, dear friends, I shall say goodbye to you now," fluted Miss Croot, after ten minutes or so.

"Thank goodness," muttered Mr Armitage.

"I am off to my new post in Siam, but I shall often think with regret of the little charges left behind, and I hope, dears, that you will all keep up the accomplishments that you have learned from me." ("They'd better not," growled her host.) "And that *you*, pets," (here she bent a severe look on the little Shepherds) "will learn some better manners. *Au revoir* to all, and *joyeux Noël.*"

At these words, the carpet beneath her feet suddenly rose and floated her out of the window.

"My carpet!" cried Mr Armitage. "My beautiful Persian carpet!"

But then they saw that the (admittedly worn) Persian carpet had been replaced by a priceless Aubusson, which, unlike Miss Croot's other gifts, did not vanish away at midnight.

All the same, it took Mr Armitage a long time to get used to it. He hated new furniture.

Three

THE BOY WHO READ ALOUD

ONCE THERE WAS a boy called Seb who was unfortunate. His dear mother had died, his father had married again, and the new wife brought in three daughters of her own. Their names were Minna, Hanna, and Morwenna, and they were all larger and older than Seb – big, fat, red-haired hateful girls. Minna pinched, Hanna tweaked hair and kicked shins, while Morwenna could pull such terrible faces that she put even the birds in a fright and her mother had forbidden her to do it indoors in case she cracked the cups and plates on the kitchen dresser. The mother was just as bad as her daughters, greedy, unkind, and such a terrible cook that nine months after they were married Seb's father wasted away and died from the food she fed him on. As for Seb, he had to manage on crusts, for that was all he got.

Now Seb had three treasures which his true mother had left him when she died. These were a little silver mug, a little silver spoon, and a book of stories. The book of stories was what he prized most, for when she was alive his true mother had read them aloud to him every day and as soon as he grew old enough to learn his letters he read them back to her while she did the ironing or peeled the potatoes or rolled out the pastry. So, now, when he opened the book, it was as if his true mother were back with him, telling him a story, and for a little he could forget how things had changed with him.

You can guess how hard Seb tried to keep these treasures hidden from his step-sisters. But they were prying, peering, poking girls, and presently Minna came across the silver cup hidden under Seb's mattress.

"You mean little sniveller, keeping this pretty cup hidden away!" she cried. "I am the eldest, it should be mine, and I'll pinch and pinch you till you give it to me!"

"For shame, Seb!" said his step-mother when she heard him crying out at the pinches. "Give the cup to your sister at once!"

So poor little Seb had to give it up.

Then Hanna found the silver spoon hidden under Seb's pillow.

"Let me have it, let me have it, you little spalpeen!" she screeched, when he tried to keep it from her. "Or I'll drag out every hair in your head."

And her mother made Seb give her the little spoon.

Now Seb took particular pains to keep his precious book out of view, hiding it first in one place and then in another, between the bins of corn, under a sitting hen, inside a hollow tree, beneath a loose floorboard. But one evening Morwenna found it tucked up on a rafter, as they were going to bed. Quickly Seb snatched the book from her and darted off to his attic room, where he shut himself in, pushing the bed against the door. Morwenna was after him in a flash – though, mind you, it was only pure spite that made her want the book for, big as she was, she could read no more than a gatepost can.

"You'd better give it to me, you little mizzler!" she bawled through the door. "Or I shall make such a fearsome face at you that you'll very likely die of fright."

Seb trembled in his shoes at this threat, but he knew that Morwenna could do nothing till morning, since she was not allowed to pull faces indoors.

Huddling in bed, clutching the book to him, he decided that the only thing for him to do was to run away. He would get up very early, climb out of the window, and slide down the roof.

But where should he go and how should he live?

For a long time, no plan came to him. But at last, remembering the book in his hands, he thought, "Well, there is one thing I can do. I can read. Perhaps somebody in the world would like me to read stories to them."

"In the village," he thought, "by the inn door, there is a board with cards stuck up on it, showing what work is to be had. I will go that way in the morning and see if anybody wants a reader."

So at last he went to sleep, holding the little book tight against his chest.

In the morning he woke and tiptoed out of the house long before anyone else was stirring. (Minna, Morwenna and Hanna were all lazy, heavy sleepers who never clambered from their beds till the sun was half across the sky.)

Seb went quietly through the garden and quietly down the village until he came to the notice-board. On it there were cards telling of jobs for gardeners, jobs for cooks, jobs for postmen, ploughmen and painters. Looking at them all he had begun to think there was nothing for him when up in the top corner he noticed a very old, dog-eared card with a bit torn off. It said:

ELDERLY BLIND RETIRED SEA
WOULD LIKE BOY TO READ
ALOUD DAILY

What a strange thing, thought Seb. Fancy reading aloud to the sea! Fancy the sea going blind at all!

But still, he supposed, thinking it over, the sea could get old like anybody else, old and blind and bored. Didn't the emperor Caligula have chats with the sea, and who takes the trouble nowadays even to pass the time of day with his neighbour, let alone have a conversation with the ocean?

There would be no harm, anyway, in going to find out whether the job had been taken already. Seb knew the way to the sea because when his true mother had been alive they had sometimes spent days at the shore. It was about twenty miles but he thought he could walk it in a couple of days. So he started at once.

Now, had Seb but known it, the truth of the matter was this: that card had been up on the board such a long time that it had been torn, and some of the words were missing. It should have read:

ELDERLY BLIND RETIRED SEA CAPTAIN
WOULD LIKE BOY TO READ NEWSPAPER
ALOUD DAILY. APPLY WITHIN.

Nobody ever had applied for the job, and in the end the sea captain had grown tired of waiting and had gone off to another town.

But Seb knew nothing of all this, so he started off to walk to the sea, with his treasured book of stories in his pocket.

It was still very early and few folk were about.

As he walked along Seb began to worry in case he had forgotten how to read aloud, because it was now a long time since his true mother had died. "I had better practise a bit," he thought.

When he had gone about five miles and felt in need of a rest he came to a gate leading into a deserted barn-yard.

"I'll go in here," he thought, "and practise my reading. Because there's no doubt about it at all, it's going to seem very queer reading to the sea till I've grown accustomed to it."

There was an old rusty Rolls-Royce car in the yard, which looked as if it had not been driven since the days when ladies wore long trailing skirts and you could get four ounces of bull's-eyes for a halfpenny. Seb felt rather sorry for the poor thing, so broken-down, forlorn and battered did it seem, and he decided to read to it.

He sat down cross-legged in front of the radiator, took out his book and read a story about the sun-god's flaming chariot, and how once it was borrowed by a boy who had not passed his driving-test, and how he drove the chariot, horses and all, into the side of a hill.

All the time Seb was reading there came no sound or movement from the car. But when he had finished and stood up to go, he was astonished to hear a toot from behind him. He turned himself about fast, wondering if somebody had been hiding in the car all the time. But it was empty, sure enough.

Then he heard a voice, which said:

"Was that a true tale, boy?"

"As to that," said Seb, "I can't tell you."

"Well, true or not," said the voice (it came from the radiator and had a sort of purring rumble to it, like the sound of a very large cat), "true or not, it was the most interesting tale I have ever heard. In fact it was the *only* tale

I have heard, and I am greatly obliged to you, boy, for reading it to me. No one else ever thought of doing such a thing. In return I will tell you something. In a well in the corner of the yard hangs a barrel of stolen money; five days ago I saw two thieves come here and lower it down. Wind the handle and you will be able to draw it up."

"Did you ever!" said Seb, and he went to the well in the corner and turned the handle which pulled the rope. Up came a barrel filled to the top with silver coins.

"There's too much here for me," Seb said. "I could never carry it all." So he took enough to fill one pocket (the book was in the other), wound the barrel down into the well again, and went on his way, waving goodbye to the Rolls-Royce car as long as he could see it.

He bought some bread with his money at the next village, and a bottle of milk.

After another five miles' walking he began to feel tired again, so he stepped aside from the road into the garden of an old empty house.

This would be a good place to read another of my stories, he thought.

So he read aloud a tale of two friends who arranged to meet one night near a hole in a wall. But they were frightened away by a lion and so they missed seeing one another.

When Seb had finished he heard a harsh voice behind him (he was sitting with his back to the house) which said:

"Was that a true tale, boy?"

"As to that," said Seb, "I can't tell you."

"True or not," said the voice, "it has given me something to think about in the long, empty days and nights. I never heard a tale before. So in return I will tell you something useful. Growing in my garden you will find a red flower which, if you pick and eat it, will cure any illness."

"But I haven't got any illness," Seb said. "I am quite well."

"If you eat this flower you will never fall ill, in the whole of your life. But take care not to pick the yellow flower which grows next it, for that is poisonous and would kill you at once."

Seb wandered through the garden until he found the red and yellow flowers growing side by side.

" 'Twould be a pity to pick the red one," he thought, "so pretty it looks growing there. Anyway I daresay somebody will come along who needs it more than I do."

So he thanked the house kindly and went on his way, waving until he was out of sight.

Presently it grew dark, so he ate some more of his bread, drank the milk, and went to sleep under an old thorn tree. Next morning, to thank the tree for watching over him all night, he read aloud a story about a girl who ran away from a suitor and turned herself into a laurel bush.

"Boy," said a rough, prickly voice when he had finished, "is that a true tale?"

"As to that," said Seb, "I don't know."

"True or not," said the voice, "I enjoyed it and it sounds

true, so I will tell you something in return. Lodged in my topmost fork is the blue stone of eternal life, which a swallow dropped there a hundred years ago. If you care to climb up you may have it. Carry it in your pocket and you will live for ever."

Seb thanked the tree and climbed up. The stone was very beautiful, dark blue, with gold marks on it and white lines. But, he said to himself, do I really want to live for ever? Why should *I* do so out of all the people in the world?

So he put the stone back in the crotch of the tree. But, unknown to him, as he turned to climb down, he dislodged the stone again and it fell into his pocket.

He went on, waving goodbye to the tree as long as it was in sight, and now he came to the sea itself, with its green waves rolling up on to the sand, each one breaking with a roar.

"Will the sea be able to hear me if I read aloud?" Seb wondered.

Feeling rather foolish, because the sea was so very large and made so much noise, he sat down on the sand. Taking out his book he read first one story and then another. At first it seemed as if nobody heard him, but then he began to hear voices, many voices, saying:

"Hush! Hush!"

And looking up he noticed that all the waves had started to smooth out as if a giant palm had flattened them, so that hardly a ripple stirred as far as he could see. The water creamed and lapped at his feet, like a dog that wants to be patted, and as he waited, not knowing whether to go on or not, a long, thin white hand came out of the green water and turned over the page.

So Seb read another story and then another.

Meanwhile what had happened at home?

When they found Seb had run away the three sisters were very angry, but specially Morwenna.

"Just let him wait till I catch him!" she said. "I'll make such a face at him that his hair turns to knitting needles."

"Oh, let him go," said the mother. "What use was he at all, but only a mouth to feed?"

None the less Morwenna and her sisters went off looking for Seb. They asked of this one and that one in the village, who had seen him, and learned that he had taken the road to the sea. So they followed after until they came to the barn-yard, and there they heard a plaintive voice wailing and sighing.

"Oh, won't some kind soul tell me a story?" it sighed. "Alack and mercy and curse it. I have such a terrible craving to hear another tale! Oh, won't somebody take pity on me?"

"Who's been telling you tales?" said Morwenna, seeing it was the old Rolls-Royce car that spoke. "Was it a little runt of a boy with a book he'd no right to sticking out of his breeches pocket? Speak the truth now, and I'll tell you another story."

"Yes, 'twas a boy," the old car said. "He read me from a wondrous book and in return I told him about the silver in the well."

"Silver in the well? Where?" screeched Minna and Hanna. Colliding together in their greed they made a rush for the well-head and wound up the handle. But Minna was so eager to get at the silver and keep her sisters from it that she jumped right on to the barrel when it came up, the rope broke, and down she went. So that was the end of Minna.

"Oh, well, never mind her," said Morwenna. "Come on, let you, for it's plain 'twas this way he went." And she hurried on, taking no notice at all of the poor old car crying out, "My story, my story!"

"Bother your story, you miserable old heap of tin!" she shouted back.

So they came to the empty house, and here again they heard a voice moaning and lamenting.

"Ochone, ochone, why did I ever listen to that boy's tale? Now I've nothing in me but an insatiable thirst to hear another."

"Was it a bit of a young boy with a little black book?" Morwenna said. "Answer me that and I'll tell you a story."

"Ah, it was, and in return for the tale he told me I showed him where to find the red flower that cures you of any sickness."

"Where is it? Where?" And the sisters went ramping through the garden till they found it. But in her haste to snatch it before her sister, Hanna grabbed the yellow flower as well, ate it, and dropped down dead on the very spot.

"Oh, well, she's done for," said Morwenna, and she hurried on, taking no notice of the old house which wailed, "My story, my story!" behind her.

"Plague take your story, you mouldy old heap of brick," she called back.

So she came to the thorn tree.

"Have you seen a boy?" she asked it. "Did he tell you a story?"

"Indeed he did, and in return I was telling him about the stone of eternal life in my topmost fork."

"Let me lay my hands on that same stone!" said Morwenna, and she made haste to scramble up the tree. But because she was such an awkward, clumsy girl she fell from the top fork in her greedy hurry, and hung head down among the thorns.

"If you'd waited a moment longer," said the tree, "I could have told you that the boy took the stone with him."

"Oh, you villainous old tree!" cried Morwenna, kicking and twisting, and making such faces as turned the birds pale in their tracks. But she was stuck fast, and hangs there to this day.

Meanwhile Seb's step-mother had married again, a man as mean-natured as she was herself. By and by they began to hear tales of a marvellous boy, who sat on the shore and read tales to the sea.

"And the sea's given him great gifts!" said one. "They say

he's been shown where the lost treasure of the Spanish galleon lies, with cups of gold and plates of pearl and wine-glasses all carved out of great rubies, and a hundred chests of silver ingots!"

"They say he's been told where every storm is, all over the world, and which way it's heading!" said another.

"They say he can listen to the voice of the sea as if it were an old friend talking to him!" said a third, "and devil a bit of a tide has there been since he began reading aloud, and a great inconvenience it is to the navigation in all realms of the world!"

"Can that boy be Seb?" wondered the step-mother and her husband. They resolved to go and see for themselves. So they harnessed up the pony-cart and made their way to the sea.

Sure enough, there on the sand was Seb, reading away from his little book. So many times he'd been through it now, he and the sea just about knew it by heart, between them.

"Why, Seb!" says his step-mother, sugar-sweet. "We've been in such an anxiety about you, child, wondering where you'd got to. Sure you'll be catching your mortal end of cold, sitting out on this great wet beach. Come home, come home, dear, for there's a grand cup of cocoa waiting for you, and a loaf with honey."

"That's very kind of you ma'am," Seb says back, all polite. "But if my sisters are there I'd just as lief not, if it's all the same to you."

"Oh, they've left," she says quickly. "So come along, dear, because the pony's beginning to fidget."

And without waiting for yea or nay she and her husband hustled Seb into the pony-cart and drove quickly home. Didn't they give him a time, then, as soon as they got in, pinching, poking and slapping one minute, buttering him up with sweet talk the next, as they tried to find out his secrets.

"Where's the sunken Spanish galleon? Where's the plates of pearl and glasses of ruby and the hundred chests of silver ingots?"

"I'm not remembering," says Seb.

"Didn't the sea tell you?"

"Sure, the sea told me one thing and another, but I was paying no heed to tales of ruby glasses and silver ingots. What do I care about silver ingots?"

"You little wretch!" she screamed. "You'd better remember, before I shake the eyes out of your head!"

"But I do remember one thing the sea told me," he says.

"What was that?"

He'd got his head turned, listening, towards the window, and he said, "The sea promised to come and help me if ever I was in trouble. And it's coming now."

Sure enough, the very next minute, every single wall of the house burst in, and the roof collapsed like an eggshell when you hit it with a spoon. There was enough sea in the garden to fill the whole Atlantic and have enough left over for the Pacific too. A great green wave lifted Seb on its shoulder and carried him out, through the garden and away, away, over the fields and hills, back to his new home among the conches and coral of the ocean bed.

As for the step-mother and her husband, they were never seen again.

But Seb is seen, it's said; sometimes at one great library, sometimes at another, you'll catch a glimpse of him, taking out longer and longer books to read aloud to his friend the sea. And so long as he keeps the blue stone in his pocket, so long he'll go on reading, and hearing wonderful secrets in return, and so long the tides will go on standing still while they listen.

Is this a true tale, you ask?

As to that, I can't tell...

Four

THE LAND OF TREES AND HEROES

THE CHILDREN HAD had whooping-cough rather badly, and although they were now well past the distressing stage of going black in the face, crowing, and having to rush from the room, they were still thin, pale, and cross. Mrs Armitage decided that they had better lose a bit more schooling and go to stay with Grandmother for a change of air. Mark and Harriet received the news listlessly. There seemed to be so many snags and prohibitions about going to Grandmother's.

"You'll have to wear your sandals all the time."

"Why, can't Granny stand noise?" asked Harriet.

"No, it's not that, but the floors are so slippery with polishing; well I remember the first time your father broke his leg coming downstairs when we were small." (The Armitage parents were cousins.) "And of course you must amuse yourselves and not bother Granny. She hasn't much time for children."

"Wouldn't it be better if we stayed at home?" Mark's tone was glum.

"No; a change is what you need. And we shall all be so busy here, with this wretched by-election." Mark's mother showed slight relief, indeed, at the thought that her children would be out of the way at this time; they had been known to upset local arrangements.

Grandmother's house was huge, old, and dark; Mark and Harriet tiptoed about in it at first like two white mice in a cave. Not that Grandmother was unkind; in her vague way she seemed pleased to see them. But after they had been staying with her for a day or two Mark and Harriet understood better what their mother had meant when she said that Granny hadn't much time for children. The old lady wasn't exactly busy, but most of the time her attention was very much elsewhere.

"Put that bayonet away, Roger," she would say absently, "How many times do I have to tell you that it will rust if you don't give it a rub when you bring it into the tent. And hang up your balaclava and ask that sepoy what he thinks he is doing."

For Granny was very, very old, and had travelled with Grandfather (dead long ago) all over the world, and seen many a battle, from Inkerman to Mafeking. She was also very deaf and seemed to understand only about a tenth part of what the children said to her as she sat knitting, placid and withdrawn, by the log fire that always burned in the great hearth. They got most of their advice and information from Nursie, who was almost as old as Grandmother, but was not at all deaf and took an active interest in their goings-on.

"Why is there a telephone in the orchard?" Harriet wanted to know.

"Ah there, Miss Harriet, dear. Always asking questions like your father before you. Why should it be there but in case your Granny wanted to ring up the orchard, then?"

"But there's nobody to answer her – only a lot of apple trees?"

"And if you're going to speak to an apple tree, better ring up than walk all that way on foot at her age," said Nursie, which only muddled Harriet more and didn't explain matters in the least. She went on thinking that it was very odd indeed to see a telephone all by itself among the trees, standing on a little pedestal in the grass with a dovecote roof over it to keep the rain off.

"And why does Granny keep all those musical things hanging in the trees if she can't hear them?"

"Ee-yolian harps, those are, Master Mark, and the others is wind-bells. And as to why she keeps them there – well, there's sounds as the ear can't hear, isn't there? Bats' squeaks, and that?"

"Yes," said Mark doubtfully.

"Well then, maybe Granny can hear those! Now run along, the pair of you, and don't bother me. Play anywhere in the garden, climb any of the trees, but don't break any branches. And don't go climbing the laurel tree or the Silver Lady will get you."

"Oh, who is the Silver Lady?"

"The Silver Lady? Why she owns the laurel tree, of course. Climb into her tree and she'll send you to sleep. There's a rhyme about it:

> "Sleep in the laurel but for an hour
> You'll sleep in the Silver Lady's power.

"So mind you keep out of it – nasty dangerous thing."

The children wanted to hear more about the Silver Lady but Nursie pushed them crossly out muttering that Silver Lady or no Silver Lady, she'd got to get her silver polished by lunch-time. They wandered into the garden shivering and forlorn, telling each other that it wasn't worth starting any game before lunch.

Many of the trees were hung with these strange Aeolian harps, or with the silvery glass bells, and it must have been a sheltered part of the country thereabouts for only very occasionally did there come a twangling and a sighing from high among the branches. Lying awake and coughing at night Mark often hoped for a wandering gust of wind-music to breathe him off to sleep but, perhaps owing to the immense thickness of the old solid walls, it was seldom that a far-off note whispered against his ear.

At five o'clock every evening Granny took off her hearing-aid and settled down to watching television; at the same time Nursie removed her thick glasses, without which she could not see more than a foot or two, and dragged her favourite upright chair close beside the wireless, turned on loud; from that minute on the two old women were quite lost to the children who would find their supper of bread-and-milk and beef tea set out on the kitchen table. The kitchen was one of the nicest rooms of the house: huge, but airy and warm with a great open range. Here they would eat, read, talk, and play a leisurely game of Ludo before taking themselves off to bed.

The nights were bad.

Their rooms were adjoining, and if Mark managed to get off to sleep for half an hour, Harriet was sure to have a shattering burst of coughing and wake him up. Then she would doze off until Mark waked her in his turn. They felt that their coughing shook the house from end to end, but of course Granny never heard them at all, and it took ages before Nursie came muttering and tutting along in her red flannel dressing-gown to give them hot drinks of lemon and barley. And sometimes, on account of her short sight and not putting on her glasses in the night-time, she rubbed their chests with the lemon barley (very sticky) and gave them hot camphorated oil to drink. Still, it was nice to have her exclaiming round them like a cross, ancient ghost, and sometimes she sang them to sleep with old, old nursery rhymes:

> "*Intery mintery, cuttery corn,*
> *Apple seed and apple thorn…*"

in her quavering, wavering voice that seemed to search round all the corners of the room before finding its note.

"Now that's enough, you must go to sleep," she would finally say severely, and at this point the children always pleaded (Harriet had come in and was sitting, wrapped in eiderdowns, on Mark's bed):

"Oh, please, the Land of Trees and Heroes before you go, please!" And Nursie would sing:

> "*In the land of Trees and Heroes*
> *The Tawny Owl is king*
> *Who locked the door, who holds the key*
> *Hidden beneath his wing.*"

"Tell us some more about the land, Nursie?"

"That's all there is, and it's time you went to sleep anyway."

They never got more than one verse out of her, which ended on a plaintive, unfinished note, but there was something about the song that made them long to know more. Where was the land? And who were the heroes? And why was the key hidden? Nursie wouldn't say.

One cold, nasty afternoon they were rummaging in the summer-house at the end of Granny's lawn and came across an old bow with a leather cover and a red velvet guard. There was a target too, but no arrows.

Mark dragged the target, moulting straw at the seams, out on to the lawn and said, "We can easily make some arrows. Never mind about feathers. Hazel's the best wood."

"Nursie said not to break any branches," Harriet reminded him doubtfully, but she rubbed her finger up and down the smooth springiness of the bow; it did seem a pity not to use it.

"Oh, she only meant big ones I expect."

They couldn't find any hazels, but there was an elder-bush growing by the summer-house with a lot of straight young branches shooting in the thick of it. Mark took out his penknife and cut two or three of these, while Harriet, to be on the safe side, politely asked the elder tree if she minded their taking this liberty. There was no reply; she had hardly expected there would be.

"They're rather light," Mark said, "but they'll do for a start."

He whittled off the leaves and twigs and cut a bow-string notch, while Harriet stood hugging her arms together, watching him.

"Now then!"

Stringing the bow he carefully fitted his arrow and fired, aiming high. The light, pithy arrow soared and began a beautiful curve towards the target, but at that moment a gentle wind sprang up and turned it sideways so that it swerved and landed in the laurel tree.

"Oh, blow!" said Mark. "That's the first wind there's been this afternoon. Hark at the wind-bells! It would happen just when I shot."

He ran towards the tree.

"Wait!" shouted Harriet, dashing after him. "What are you doing?"

"Going to get the arrow."

"But don't you remember – the Silver Lady!"

"Heavens, I'm not going to stay in the tree an hour! It won't take two twos to nip up and get the arrow. I can see it from here."

"Do be careful…" She arrived at the tree just as he swung himself into the centre crotch, and stood with her hands on the trunk anxiously looking up at him.

"I can almost reach it now," he called in a moment from somewhere in the middle of the tree. "Goodness, there's a cat up here – it seems to be fast asleep! And a whole lot of birds, asleep too. How peculiar."

"Oh do hurry up!"

"And here's a satchel." Mark's voice was muffled now by the thick green leaves among which he was scuffling and flapping. "Good Lord, I say, there's a postman asleep up here – I never saw him climb up, did you? And there's something that looks like a butcher's basket full of chops. This is the oddest tree I've ever bee…" His voice trailed away on a tremendous yawn.

"Mark!" shouted Harriet, her voice sharp with anxiety.

No answer.

"Mark!" Twisting her head she peered about, looking into the dark cave of the tree. And then she saw Mark. He was fourteen or fifteen feet up, curled comfortably into a fork as if he were lying in a hammock, and he was fast asleep, his head pillowed on his hand. In the fork above him was a tabby cat, also fast asleep, and over to the left she could dimly make out a butcher's boy in a striped blue and white apron, sleeping wedged in a nest of criss-crossing branches.

Harriet shouted till she was hoarse, and shook the tree till she started herself coughing, but there was no reply from any of the sleepers.

"Oh goodness," she said to herself miserably, "I knew something like this would happen. Now what had I better do?"

Telling Nursie seemed the first step, and she went indoors. But five o'clock had struck and Nursie was listening to a programme of Young Artists from the Midlands, and was not to be disturbed. She waved Harriet away with a preoccupied hand.

"If I don't get Mark out of the tree before the hour's up," thought Harriet, "I don't know how we shall ever wake him. I wonder if I could drag him down?"

She went back to the tree but decided this would be too risky; Mark was too heavy for her to lift, even on to a ladder, and if he fell from that height he would probably break a leg. Besides, something ought to be done about the postman and the butcher's boy too, she felt; goodness knew how long they had been there. And she certainly couldn't manage *them*.

"I know," she decided, "I'll go for the doctor."

Dr Groves lived a little way up the lane. They had been to see him when they arrived, for a check-over, and had liked him very much.

"He'll be able to help," Harriet thought.

She ran round to the shed by the stables and got out Nursie's bicycle; this was no time for loitering. Without waiting to ask for permission, Harriet sped off down the front path and took the steps at a slither. Thank goodness it was not a surgery night, and Dr Groves was sitting by his fire, peacefully reading the *Lancet*, when Harriet arrived, panting and gasping, about three minutes later.

"Please will you help me," she wheezed, trying not to cough. "Mark's gone to sleep up the laurel tree."

"Eh, dear, has he now," said Dr Groves. "And you want me to help pull him down, is that it?"

"Yes please. And there are two other people in the tree, and a cat. I expect they ought to come down too."

"Tut, tut." The doctor sounded more disapproving than surprised. "And what would they have been doing up there, I wonder?"

"I don't know. One of them's the postman. Oh please hurry."

"I can't hurry much, my lass, on account of my leg. Eh, well now, the postman. We all wondered where he'd got to when he vanished last May." He pulled himself stiffly to his feet and Harriet remembered with dismay that he had an artificial leg.

"Should I get somebody else?" she said anxiously. "Will it be too much for you?"

"No, no, I'll manage very well. Just pass me that stick, will you, lass?"

They made slow progress down the lane, and Harriet did rings round the doctor in her impatience to get on.

"Ah, it's a great convenience to me, this leg," he said imperturbably, as he clanked along. "Bitten off by a shark, it was, in the days when I was a bold, buccaneering sea-doctor, and I fitted myself up with the best cast-iron peg I could lay hands on. I can use it for poking the fire or bowling over a charging tiger – and best of all, when some fussing woman gets a pain in her little finger and thinks of sending for the doctor she thinks again and says to herself, 'With his leg it'll take him an hour and twenty minutes to get here, it's not worth fetching him out,' and that saves me a great, great deal of trouble, I can tell you, for I'm a lazy old man with no wish to do two trips when one will do."

"Oh yes, I'm sure it does," said Harriet, wheeling round him distractedly. "Are you sure you wouldn't like to ride Nursie's bicycle?"

"No, thank you, my bairn. Riding a bicycle is one of the things I can *not* do with this leg. But we're managing very well, very well indeed."

Dusk was falling as he stumped up Granny's steps, and Harriet looked at her watch and saw with a sinking heart that it had taken them forty-five minutes to do the return journey; Mark must have been in the laurel tree for very nearly an hour.

"Ah yes, there they are," said Dr Groves, pulling a flashlight from his pocket and shining it up into the tree. "Fast asleep, the three of them. And Pussie baudrons too, after birds, nae doubt, the naughty grimalkin. And that's an interesting thing, very interesting indeed, that the laurel tree should have such soporific power. When I was a boy I would always use laurel leaves for putting butterflies to sleep. In a jam-jar."

Without listening to his reflections, which seemed likely to go on for ever, Harriet dashed off and came back with Granny's aluminium fruit-picking ladder, which she planted firmly against the trunk.

Dr Groves had embarked on a learned chat with himself about the medical properties of various plants, so she started up the ladder, saying over her shoulder:

"If I pull them down, Dr Groves, do you think you can catch them?"

"I'll do my best, lass. Feet first is the way, feet first, now. Don't let the poor slumberers fall on their heads, or you'd do better to leave them bide where they are."

The butcher's boy was the nearest, and Harriet tugged him down cautiously, being most careful herself not to get into the tree even for a moment. Dr Groves received the long dangling legs and flopped the boy on to the ground, where he lay limp and sprawling. Harriet dropped his basket of chops (they flew in all directions) and moved the ladder round to Mark, who was more difficult to shift: half lifting, half dragging, she at last managed to get him clear of the branches and lower him to the doctor. He was laid unceremoniously among the chops while they tackled the postman, who was the most troublesome of all. In the end

Harriet had to get the clothes-line and make a very unseamanlike hitch round his shoulders so that she could let him bumpingly down to the doctor. She herself had to come down from time to time for a breath of fresh air; even perched on the ladder she found that she felt uncommonly sleepy.

"I can't reach the cat and I'm not going to risk being caught by the Silver Lady for a lot of starlings," she said, descending for the last time. "What shall we do with them now?"

"Eh well, there's little can be done till I've reflected," said the doctor, who seemed to be infected by the general somnolence and was yawning dreadfully. "We'll just get them indoors safe and snug and then I'll be off home. I'll come down in the morning for a confabulation with your Granny. Meanwhile they'll take no harm."

Using the wheelbarrow they carted the slumberers into a sort of garden-room, where they left them propped about in canvas swings and deck-chairs, covered with tartan rugs. The rising moon silvered the three inert bundles through the window as Harriet and the doctor stepped out, closing the glass door behind them, and the doctor's peg-legged shadow stretched out, long and fantastic, across the misty lawn, as he stumped off with a good-night wave.

Harriet turned indoors, feeling rather forlorn. She didn't want any supper and went straight upstairs to bed. The whole house was as quiet as a stringless harp and she missed Mark's coughing from next door. Nevertheless she managed to fall asleep and drifted into some very strange dreams about flying cats, laurel trees full of sharks, and a Silver Lady with a wooden leg. "You give me back my brother!" shouted Harriet, and at once became aware that she was coughing, and that she was awake.

"Eh, nonny, nonny, what's all this?" said Nursie, materializing beside the bed with her candle and red dressing-gown. "Here you are then, my duck, here's a drink of blackcurrant for that cough." Harriet obediently swallowed it down. It tasted like permanganate.

"Nursie," she said miserably, "we've lost Mark. The Silver Lady's got him. He's asleep and won't wake up."

"Laws-a-me," said Nursie sharply, "he's been up the laurel tree then? All the same, they are – tell them not to do a thing and they run straight away and do it. A good sleep'll work wonders for his cough, that's one comfort."

"But how are we going to wake him? The postman's been asleep since May."

"As to that," Nursie answered, "I couldn't say. The rhyme says:

"Those by the silver slumber taken
Only the Tawny Owl can waken.

"But I can hear a tawny owl down in the orchard this minute and it would take more than that to wake Master Mark in the normal way, let alone when the Silver Lady's put her finger on his lips. We'll think about it in the morning, Miss Harriet dear. I must be off now and answer the telephone, drat it, at half-past nine of the night."

The telephone was the children's father, ringing up to ask if they were behaving themselves. Nursie told him to hold on while she fetched Granny from the television. On the way she told Granny what had happened to Mark.

"That you, Mother? How are you?" shouted Mr Armitage, loud enough to penetrate Granny's deafness.

"I am well, thank you, Geoffrey, I can hear perfectly well over the telephone. Mark is unfortunately in a coma; the fault of the Silver Lady, you know; otherwise nothing out of the common has occurred."

"What? What?" shouted Mr Armitage, becoming very agitated. "What are you doing about it?"

"Why, my dear boy, there is nothing to be done. It is my bedtime now, good night."

And Granny firmly rang off, leaving Mr Armitage in a great state of irritation. The dying tink of the telephone came to Harriet as she lay awake and worrying in a patch of moonlight. Something ought to be done about Mark soon, she was sure, otherwise he might sink into so deep a sleep that he could *never* be woken. And then all their plans for Christmas would be spoiled. Not to mention Easter.

The Tawny Owl, Nursie had said. There was a tawny owl, too, in the rhyme about the trees and heroes. Perhaps it was the same one? In any case the time to find a tawny owl was now, while it was dark and the owls were abroad, not tomorrow morning when they were all fast asleep and hidden away in thickets.

Harriet had by now thought herself wide awake, and she got up silently and began putting on her clothes. The sound of the telephone had given her an idea. It seemed so wild and odd that she hardly liked to put it to herself in actual thought, but she slipped out of her room, carrying her shoes in her hand, and went downstairs to the little telephone room off the front hall. The house was silent again. Nursie and Granny had gone to bed. Only the faint crackle of coal came from the kitchen stove settling for the night.

Harriet sat looking at the telephone in its little pool of moonlight. How did you ring up an orchard? In the end she dialled O.

For a long, long time she could hear ringing and nobody answered. She almost gave up in despair and put the receiver back, but then she thought she might as well wait a bit longer. At last the ringing sound stopped, there came a click, and she could hear a far-off sighing, like the wind in the branches.

"Who is there?" she asked rather nervously.

A whisper answered her. "Cox's Orrrr-range Pippin speeee-king," it murmured leafily against her ear. "To whooooooom did you wissssssssh to speeeeeeeeeak?"

"May I please speak to the Tawny Owl?" Harriet's heart beat in triumph at this success.

"Hold on, pleasssss..." whispered Cox's Orange, and there was another long pause, a long, long pause, while

Harriet heard, down the receiver, the trees in the orchard all turning their branches this way and that against the night sky.

Presently there came a click as if somebody had picked up the receiver.

"I – is that the Tawny Owl?" Harriet asked.

"Who?"

"I asked to speak to the Tawny Owl."

"To who?"

"You mean, to whom," Harriet was on the point of saying, when she realized that it *was* the Tawny Owl speaking. She explained the trouble they were in, and that he was their only hope. "Oh, please, sir," she ended despairingly, "won't you help us? I'm sure Dr Groves won't have much idea what to do."

"You will need ammunition," said the Tawny Owl. "To wit, a bow and some arrows."

"I can manage that." Harriet was much encouraged by his voice – a friendly, brown, furry sort of voice. "What shall I do?"

"Bring them to the laurel tree. Do not delay. I shall be there."

"Oh, *thank* you," Harriet said gratefully.

"Who?"

"You – oh, I mean whoo," she replied politely, put the receiver back and ran tiptoeing to the garden-room where she had left the bow and the remaining two arrows. Everyone was breathing peacefully and she went out, making snail-tracks in the moony dew, across the lawn to the laurel tree.

She had not been there a moment when the branches parted and a large pale shape coasted silently down and landed as lightly as a dead leaf on her shoulder. She felt the smoothness of feathers against her cheek.

"Whooo," the Tawny Owl said gently in her ear. "The arrows – of what wood are they?"

"Elder."

"A moody personality. Was permission obtained? It would not do to be rude to her."

"We – we asked," said Harriet anxiously. "But she didn't answer."

"I will inquire anew. Do you procure a bicycle and return hither – be swift. Adieu."

Quick as she was, he had returned to the tree before her.

"Elder is graciously pleased to allow the use of those two. It is a propitious wood. Now! We must go fast. I will instruct you as to the route."

He found that it was best if he flew ahead and Harriet followed. Whizzing after him down the garden path she realized that she was not going to have time to dismount for the steps, and she discovered without much surprise halfway down them that she had become airborne and was pedalling briskly after the owl ten feet above the white surface of the road, which streamed away like a nylon ribbon beneath.

"Where are we going?" she called after him.

"To the Land," his hoot came faintly back between wing-beats, "to the Land of Trees and Heroes..."

It was a wonderful ride. Harriet would not have minded going on all night, seeing the moon-silvered fields sliding under her feet and breathing the sharp cold scent of the trees when they swooped through the darkness of a wood. But presently she found that they were toiling up a long, cloudy ascent; the Tawny Owl went more slowly and she herself was glad of Nursie's three-speed. Great cliffs of cloud built up on either side, drifts of loose mist sometimes obscured the path, and at length they came to a door.

The owl flew up against it and clung, like a woodpecker to the side of a tree, and in a moment or two the door opened and they passed through.

Harriet often wished afterwards that she had had more time to notice the beauties of that land. It was smooth and rolling: a country like a counterpane of grassy downs with small groves on the hilltops, set with statues that shone white, here and there, against the trees.

Strolling on the grass or lying in the shade, some near, some far, were the heroes. Many of them Harriet recognized at once. There was Hercules, doing his best, with the assistance of two grass-snakes, to copy the position of a statue of himself, but the snakes were not being very co-operative. There was Jason with only one sandal. There was Prince Hal, galloping about on a fiery horse chasing Ivanhoe; Davy Crockett and Robin Hood having a shooting match; Captain Nemo and Captain Ahab chatting in the shade. Harriet saw with wonder, not unmixed with envy, that the postman was with them, that the butcher's boy was playing bowls with Drake and Raleigh, and that Bellerophon was giving Mark a ride on Pegasus.

"How did they get here?" she asked in astonishment.

"They dream," the Tawny Owl answered her. She had propped her bicycle against an ilex tree and he was once more sitting on her shoulder. "But now you must not delay – the Silver Lady will soon be returning and you must shoot her."

"I don't much want to shoot anybody," Harriet said doubtfully.

"She will take no harm from it. And only thus will you have power over her. Watch now…"

"String your bow," said Robin Hood, who had strolled up and stood watching with friendly interest. "Then you'll be ready. Like this…"

Several other heroes gathered round with encouragement and advice as Harriet pointed her bow at the sky. Bellerophon grounded Pegasus in case of accidents. "Isn't this a grand place," Mark shouted to Harriet.

"There she goes!" suddenly came a cry from the watchers, and Harriet saw something silvery and unbelievably swift streak across the sky towards the moon.

"Quick," the Tawny Owl murmured, "before she hides. Or you will have to wait for twenty-four hours."

Harriet shot after the flashing figure.

"Oh!" came a long-drawn cry from the watchers. "You've shot the moon!"

And so indeed she had. Down it came tumbling and drifting, like a great silver honesty-pod falling through leaves of air. All the shadows rushed upward.

Harriet was appalled. But Ivanhoe, galloping to where the moon lay blazing coldly, shouted, "You've caught her!"

"Make haste!" called Jason.

Harriet ran to the moon. It had fallen on its edge and was standing upright, like a half-crown the size of a nursery table. The arrow, thrust clean through, was still quivering. And on the far side of the moon the Silver Lady struggled angrily to be free. The arrow had caught the bracelet on her wrist and she was a prisoner, fastened by one hand to the shining disc. She was very beautiful, but her rage was frightening and Harriet hesitated before approaching her; the air all round her was freezingly cold.

"Don't be afraid," said the Tawny Owl in her ear, and he called to the lady, "Mistress, the child has beaten you fairly."

"Not without your help and counsel," the Silver Lady replied, giving him a black look. "Well, child, what is it you want? Quick! Selene is not to be humiliated for long."

"I – I want you to set my brother free, please," Harriet said hurriedly, "and the postman and butcher's boy."

"Is that all? You might have asked for kingdoms while you were about it." And the lady blew in the direction of Mark, who vanished like a pricked bubble. The postman and butcher's boy disappeared at the same time. Then, twitching her bracelet free from the arrow, the lady smiled at Harriet enchantingly and shot upwards like a spark to the Milky Way.

"You must put back the moon," she called over her shoulder, "or you will be my next prisoner."

Put back the moon! Harriet stared at it in horror. How was that to be done? But Perseus grinned at her reassuringly, tugged it out of the ground and, leaning backwards, slung it up with a mighty swing of his arm. Higher and higher it soared, and finally steadied, like a kite that feels the pull of the wind, and sailed among its accustomed stars.

"Homeward now," the owl warned Harriet. "Dawn approaches."

It was a race home, through the mighty door, down the slopes of paling cloud. The stars were thinning as they covered the last furlong, and the bearings on Nursie's bicycle were red hot.

"Owl," said Harriet when they stood again below the laurel tree, "is the tree disenchanted now?"

"Oh no," said the owl, "the tree is Selene's, and will always be hers. Just as the other trees in your Grandmother's garden each belong to a different power. Did you not know? The Elder, the Quince, and the dark-berried Yew..." His voice was trailing away as if he were yawning and he murmured "Adieu" and gave Harriet's ear a little peck just as the sun rose and he flitted silently off to a lilac-thicket.

Harriet watched him go with regret. There were so many things she wanted to ask.

"There!" Nursie clucked in triumph at breakfast. "Didn't I say a night's rest would break the spell?"

"No," Harriet said, but she yawned as she said it, and the clatter of knives and forks drowned her voice anyway. Mark, the postman and the butcher's boy were eating an enormous breakfast. In the middle of it Dr Groves stumped in and heard their tale with interest and envy.

"Did ye now? Do they now?" he exclaimed at intervals as they compared notes and Mark told Harriet how he had gone chariot-racing with Phoebus and Boadicea. "Well, something has cured your cough at all events, whether the sleep or the change of air."

It was true. Mark had not coughed once since he woke, though Harriet still had a fit of it from time to time.

"It is unfair!" she exclaimed. "When I had all the trouble of fetching him back."

They had been arguing about this for some minutes when they noticed that the doctor and the postman had left the room. Glancing out of the window Harriet saw them cross the lawn to the laurel tree. The ladder was still leaning against it and now, helped by the postman, the doctor hauled himself up with surprising agility and disappeared into the branches. The postman followed him.

"Hey!" Harriet shouted, leaning from the window, "that's dangerous! It's still enchanted..."

But they were gone, and when the children ran out and stood under the tree they could hear only contented snores coming from the upper branches.

Five

THE COST OF NIGHT

THERE WAS ONCE a king called Merrion the Carefree who was inclined to be foolish. Perhaps this was because his wife had died when her baby daughter was born some years before, and so there was no one to keep an eye on the king. His worst failing was that he could never resist a game of chance; but of course all his subjects knew about this, and none of them would have dreamed of suggesting a game.

However it happened once that the king was returning home after a visit to a distant province of his kingdom. Towards twilight he came to a great river that was swift-flowing and wide. As he hesitated on the brink, for he was but an indifferent swimmer, he saw, moving through the reeds, an enormously large crocodile, with teeth as big as tenpins, cold expressionless yellow eyes, and a skin that looked as old and wrinkled and horny as the world itself.

"Ho, crocodile!" said King Merrion. "I am your lord and ruler, Merrion the Carefree, so it is plainly your duty to turn crossways over the river and make a bridge, in order that I may walk dry-shod from bank to bank."

At this the crocodile gave a great guttural choking bark, which might have been either a sardonic laugh or a respectful cough.

"Ahem, Your Majesty! I am no subject of yours, being indeed a traveller like yourself, but out of courtesy and good fellowship I don't mind making a bridge across the river for you, on one condition: that you play a game of heads or tails with me."

Now at this point, of course, the king should have had the sense to draw back. Better if he had slept all night on the bank, or travelled upstream till he came to the next bridge, however far off it lay. But he was tired, and eager to be home; besides, at the notion of a game, all sense and caution fled out of his head.

"I'll be glad to play with you, crocodile," he said. "But only one quick game, mind, for I am already late and should have been home hours ago."

So the crocodile, smiling all the way along his hundred teeth, turned sideways-on, and King Merrion walked on his horny back dry-shod from one river-bank to the other. Although the crocodile's back was covered in mud it was not slippery because of all the wrinkles.

When the king had stepped right over the hundred-tooth smile and off the crocodile's long muddy snout, he looked about him and picked up a flat stone which was white on one side and brown on the other.

"This will do for our game, if you agree," he said.

"Certainly I agree," said the crocodile, smiling more than ever.

"What shall we play for?"

"The loser must grant the winner any gift he asks. You may throw first," the crocodile said politely.

So the king threw, and the crocodile snapped, "White!" Sure enough, the stone landed white side up.

Then the crocodile threw, and the king called, "Brown!" But again the stone landed white side up.

Then the king threw, and again the crocodile said "White!" and the stone landed white side up. For the fact of the matter was that the crocodile was not a genuine crocodile at all, but a powerful enchanter who chose to appear in that shape.

So the crocodile guessed right every time, and the king guessed wrong, until he was obliged to acknowledge that he had lost the game.

"What do you want for your gift?" said he.

The crocodile smiled hugely, until he looked like a tunnel through the Rocky Mountains.

"Give me," he said, "all the dark in your kingdom."

At this the king was most upset. "I am not sure that the dark is mine to give away," he said. "I would rather that you had asked me for all the gold in my treasury."

"What use is gold to me?" said the crocodile.

"Remember your kingly word. The dark I want, and the dark I must have."

"Oh, very well," said the king, biting his lip. "If you must, you must."

So the crocodile opened his toothy mouth even wider, and sucked, with a suction stronger than the widest whirlpool, and all the dark in King Merrion's kingdom came rushing along and was sucked down his great cavernous throat. Indeed he sucked so hard that he swallowed up, not only the dark that covered King Merrion's country, but the dark that lay over the entire half of the world facing away from the sun, just as you might suck the pulp off a ripe plum. And he smacked his lips over it, for dark was his favourite food.

"That was delicious!" he said. "Many thanks, Majesty! May your shadow never grow less!"

And with another loud harsh muddy laugh he disappeared.

King Merrion went home to his palace, where he found everyone in the greatest dismay and astonishment. For instead of there being night, as would have been proper at that time, the whole country was bathed in a strange unearthly light, clear as day, but a day in which nothing cast any shadow. Flowers which had shut their petals opened them again, birds peevishly brought their heads out from under their wings, owls and bats, much puzzled, returned to their thickets, and the little princess Gudrun refused to go to bed.

Indeed, after a few days, the unhappy king realized that he had brought a dreadful trouble to his kingdom – and to the whole world – by his rash promise. Without a regular spell of dark every twelve hours, nothing went right – plants grew tall and weak and spindly, cattle and poultry became confused and stopped producing milk and eggs, winds gave up blowing, and the weather went all to pieces. As for people, they were soon in a worse muddle than the cows and hens. At first everybody tried to work all night, so as to make the most of this extra daylight, but they soon became cross and exhausted and longed for rest. However it was almost impossible to sleep, for no matter what they did, covering their windows with thick curtains, shutting their doors, hiding under the bedclothes and bandaging their eyes, not a scrap of dark could anybody find. The crocodile had swallowed it all.

As for the children, they ran wild. Bed-time had ceased to exist.

The little princess Gudrun was the first to become tired of such a state of affairs. She was very fond of listening to stories, and what she enjoyed almost more than anything else was to lie in bed with her eyes tight shut in the warm dark, and remember the fairy-tales that her nurse used to tell her. But in the hateful daylight that went on and on it was not possible to do this. So she went to confide in her greatest friend and ask his service.

Gudrun's greatest friend was a great black horse called Houniman, a battle-charger who had been sent as a gift to

King Merrion several years before; battles were not very frequent at that time, so Houniman mostly roamed, grazing the palace meadows. Now Gudrun sought him out, and gave him a handful of golden corn, and tried to pretend, by burying her face in his long, thick black mane, that the dark had come again.

"What shall we do about it, Houniman?" she said.

"It is obviously no use expecting your silly father to put matters right," Houniman replied.

"No, I am afraid you are right," Gudrun said, sighing.

"So, as he has given away all the dark in the entire world, we shall have to find out where dark comes from and how we can get some more of it."

"But who," she said, "would know such a thing?"

Houniman considered, "If we travel towards Winter," he said at length, "perhaps we might learn something, for in winter the dark grows until it almost swallows up the light."

"Good," said the princess, "let us travel towards Winter." So she fetched a woolly cloak, and filled her pockets with bread and cheese, and brought a bag of corn for Houniman, and they started out. Nobody noticed them go, since all the people in the kingdom were in such a state of muddle and upset, and King Merrion worst of all.

The princess rode on Houniman and he galloped steadily northwards for seven days and what ought to have been seven nights, over a sea of ice, until they came to the Land of Everlasting Winter, where the words freeze as you speak them, and even thoughts rattle in your head like icicles.

There they found the Lord of Winter, in the form of a great eagle, brooding on a rock.

"Sir," called Gudrun from a good way off – for it was so cold in his neighbourhood that the very birds froze in the air and hung motionless – can you tell us where we can find a bit of dark?"

He lifted his head with its great hooked beak and gave them an angry look.

"Why should I help you? I have only one little piece of dark, and I am keeping it for myself, under my wing, so that it may grow."

"Does dark grow?" said Gudrun.

"Of course it grows, stupid girl! Cark! Be off with you!" And the eagle spread one wing (keeping the other tight folded) so that a great white flurry of snow and wind drove towards Gudrun and Houniman, and they turned and galloped away.

At the edge of the Land of Winter they saw an old woman leading a reindeer loaded with wood.

"Mother," called Gudrun, "can you tell us where we might find a bit of dark?"

"Give me a piece of bread and cheese for myself and some corn for my beast and I will consider."

So they gave her the bread and corn and she considered. Presently she said:

"There will be plenty of dark in the past. You should go

to No Man's Land, the frontier where the present slips into the past, and perhaps you might be able to pick up a bit of dark there."

"Good," said the princess, "that sounds hopeful. But in which direction does the past lie?"

"Towards the setting sun, of course!" snapped the old woman, and she gave her reindeer a thump to make it jog along faster.

So Gudrun and Houniman turned towards the setting sun and galloped on for seven days and what should have been seven nights, until they reached No Man's Land. This was a strange and misty region, with low hills and marshes; in the middle of it they came to a great lake, on the shore of which sat an old poet in a little garden of cranberry shrubs. Instead of water the lake was filled with blue-grey mist, and the old poet was drawing out the mist in long threads, and twisting them and turning them into poems. It was very silent all around there, with not a living creature, and the old poet was so absorbed in what he did that he never lifted his head until they stood beside him.

"Can you tell us, uncle poet," said Gudrun, "where we might pick up a bit of dark?"

"Dark?" he said absently. "Eh, what's that? You want a bit of dark? There's plenty at the bottom of the lake."

So Gudrun dismounted and walked to the edge of the lake, and looked down through the mist. Thicker and thicker it grew, darker and darker, down in the depths of the lake, and as she looked down she could see all manner of strange shapes, and some that seemed familiar too – faces that she had once known, places that she had once visited, all sunk down in the dark depths of the past. As she leaned over, the mist seemed to rise up around her, so that she began to become sleepy, to forget who she was and what she had come for...

"Gudrun! Come back!" cried Houniman loudly, and he stretched out his long neck and caught hold of her by the hair and pulled her back, just as she was about to topple into the lake.

"Climb on my back and let's get out of here!" he said. "Dark or no dark, this place is too dangerous!"

But Gudrun cried to the poet, "Uncle poet, isn't there any other place where we might pick up a bit of dark?"

"Dark?" he said. "You want a bit of dark? Well, I suppose you might try the Gates of Death; dark grows around there."

"Where are the Gates of Death?"

"You must go to the middle of the earth, where the sky hangs so low that it is resting on the ground, and the rivers run uphill. There you will find the Gates of Death."

And he went back to his poem-spinning.

So they galloped on for seven days and what should have been seven nights, until the mountains grew higher and higher, and the sky hung lower and lower, and at last they came to the Gates of Death.

This place was so frightening that Gudrun's heart went

small inside her, because everything seemed to be turning into something else. The sky was dropping into the mountains, and the mountains piercing into the sky. A great river ran uphill, boiling, and in front of the Gates of Death themselves a huge serpent lay coiled, with one yellow eye half open, watching as they drew near.

"Cousin serpent," called Gudrun, trying not to let her teeth chatter, "can you tell us where we might pick up a little piece of dark?"

"Ssss! Look about you, stupid girl!" hissed the serpent.

When Gudrun looked about her she saw that the ground was heaving and shuddering as if some great live creature were buried underneath, and there were cracks and holes in the rock, through which little tendrils of dark came leaking out.

But as fast as they appeared, the serpent snapped them off and gobbled them up.

Gudrun stretched out her hand to pick an uncurling frond of dark.

"Sssstop!" hissed the serpent, darting out his head till she drew back her hand in a fright. "All this dark is mine! And since my brother the crocodile ate all the dark in the world I will not part with one sprig of it, unless you give me something in return."

"But what can I give you?" said Gudrun, trembling.

"You can give me your black horse. He is the colour of night, he will do very well for a tasty bite. Give him to me and you may pick one sprig of dark."

"No, no, I cannot give you Houniman," cried Gudrun weeping. "He belongs to my father, not to me, and besides, he is my friend! I could not let him suffer such a dreadful fate. Take me instead, and let Houniman carry the dark back to my father's kingdom."

"*You* wouldn't do at all," hissed the serpent. "You have golden hair and blue eyes, you would give me indigestion. No, it must be the horse, or I will not part with any dark. But you must take off his golden shoes, or they will give me hiccups."

And Houniman whispered to the princess, "Do as the serpent says, for I have a notion that all will come right. But take care to keep my golden shoes."

So Gudrun wiped the tears from her eyes and Houniman lifted each foot in turn while she pulled off his golden shoes. And she put them in her pockets while the serpent sucked with a great whistling noise and sucked in Houniman, mane, tail and all.

Then Gudrun picked one little sprig of dark and ran weeping away from the Gates of Death. She ran on until she was tired, and then she turned and looked back. What was her horror to see that the serpent had uncoiled himself and was coming swiftly after her. "For," he had thought to himself, "I merely told her that she could *pick* one sprig in exchange for the horse, I did not say that she could carry it away. It would be a pity to waste a good sprig." So he was coming over the rocky ground, faster than a horse could gallop.

Quick as thought, Gudrun took one of the gold

horseshoes out of her pocket and flung it so that it fell over the serpent, pinning him to the rock. Twist and writhe as he might, he could not get free, and she was able to run on until he was left far behind.

She passed through No Man's Land, but she was careful not to go too near the lake of mist. And she passed through the Land of Everlasting Winter, where the eagle sat guarding his little bit of dark. Then she came to the sea of ice, but now spring was coming, and the ice was beginning to melt.

"How shall I get over to the sea?" Gudrun wondered. "Oh, how I wish my dear Houniman were here to advise me."

But then she remembered the gold horseshoes and thought they might help. So she pulled another from her pocket, and directly she did so it spread and stretched and turned into a boat. So Gudrun stepped into it, all the time hugging the little spring of dark carefully against her heart, and the boat carried her safe across the sea.

Then she came to the borders of her father's kingdom, but it was still a long and weary way to his palace. For the journey that on Houniman's back had lasted only three times seven days and what should have been nights, took much longer on foot, and it was almost a year since she had left the Gates of Death. But the little sprig of dark had been growing and growing all the time.

Now Gudrun came to a wide, swift river.

In the reeds by the edge lay a crocodile, and he watched her approach with his yellow expressionless eyes.

"Ho there, little princess," he said. "I will play a game of heads or tails with you. If you win, I will turn my length across the river to make a bridge for you. And if I win, you shall give me the sprig of dark that you carry."

But Gudrun did not share her father's fondness for games of chance.

"Thank you," she said to the crocodile, "but I have a bridge of my own."

And she took out her third horseshoe, which immediately grew into a golden bridge, over which she crossed, leaving the crocodile to gnash his teeth with rage.

Gudrun ran on, slower and slower, for by now she was very tired, and the sprig of dark she carried had grown to the size of a young tree. But at last she reached her father's palace, and all the people ran out, with King Merrion in front, clapping their hands for joy.

"She has brought back the dark! Our darling princess has brought back the dark!"

"You must plant it in a safe, warm place and cherish it," said Gudrun faintly. "For I am afraid that the serpent and the crocodile may still come after it."

So it was planted in the palace garden, and it slowly grew bigger and bigger – first as big as a nut tree, then big as a young birch, then big as a spreading oak. And King Merrion's subjects took turns to guard it, and Gudrun stayed beside it always.

But one day the envious crocodile came creeping along, in the shadow thrown by the tree of dark. The man set to guard the tree was almost asleep, for the shadow made him drowsy after so many months of daylight, but Gudrun saw the crocodile.

Quick as a flash she pulled out her fourth horseshoe and threw it, pinning the crocodile to the ground.

But then she grew very anxious. "For," she said, "what shall we do if the serpent comes? Now I have no more horseshoes! Oh, my dear, good, faithful friend Houniman, how I do miss you!"

And she laid her head against the trunk of the tree and wept bitter tears.

Now this watering was just what the tree needed, and that very minute it grew and flourished until its branches spread right across the sky and true night had come at last. Directly this happened, all the creatures of night who had stayed sulking in their hiding-places for so long, the owls and moths and night-herons, the bats, bitterns, nightjars and nightingales, and all the beasts of darkness, came out rejoicing and calling down blessings on the little princess Gudrun. But she still knelt weeping beside the tree.

Then the king of the night creatures, who was an enormous owl, looked down with his great eyes and saw the serpent creeping through the dark. (In the end, after many days, he had managed to wriggle out from under the horseshoe.)

"Thief, thief!" cried the owl. "Kill him! Kill him!" And all the creatures of dark flew down, pecking and tearing, until they had pecked the serpent into a thousand pieces.

And out of the pieces sprang Houniman, alive and well!

Then Gudrun flung her arms round Houniman's neck and wept for joy, and King Merrion offered him any reward he cared to name for helping to bring back dark to the world.

"All I ask," said Houniman, "is that you set me free, for in my own land, far to the east, where night begins, I was king and lord over all the wild horses."

"Willingly will I grant what you ask," said King Merrion. So Houniman was given his freedom and he bade a loving farewell to the princess Gudrun and galloped away and away, home to his own country. But he sent back his son, the black colt Gandufer, to be the princess's lifelong companion and friend.

The creatures of the night offered to peck the crocodile to pieces too, but King Merrion said no to that.

"I shall keep him a prisoner always, and the sight of him will be a reminder to me never again to get mixed up in a game of chance!" he said.

And so this was done.

Six

THE STOLEN QUINCE TREE

HARRIET WAS SITTING alone upstairs in the dormer window over the porch. There was an old basket-chair and a shelf full of entrancing books: *Jackanapes*, *The Silver Skates*, the Curdie books, and many others with thick, glossy old bindings and gold lettering. The afternoon sun shone in and made a pinkish patch on the floor. Harriet felt drowsy and comfortable. The remains of whooping-cough were still troublesome and kept her awake at nights; Granny had said that she must rest for at least an hour after lunch from two to three. She was resting now, while Mark practised archery somewhere in the garden.

Granny had gone off to call on Mrs Cheevy and Nursie was at her weekly W.I. meeting, so Harriet was in command. It was nice, she thought, to hear the aged house stretching itself and creaking a little round her; the only thing she did wish was that Granny kept a cat, a comfortable tabby or marmalade to stretch beside her in the patch of sunshine and let out a friendly purr from time to time.

Cars passed occasionally in the lane below Granny's ten brick front steps, but they never stopped. All Granny's friends were very, very old now, and exchanged letters with her in crabbed trembling handwritings, but they never came calling. Now, however, to Harriet's surprise, a large glossy car did draw up outside the white gate and a lady jumped out of it and came purposefully up the steps, calling back a remark to someone in the car as she did so.

Oh bother, Harriet thought, now the bell will ring and I shall have to answer it.

She waited. The bell rang.

Uncoiling herself with reluctance from the squeaking chair (which had left basket-marks all over her legs) she went down the stairs, absent-mindedly stepping over the patch of sunshine where the cat should have been lying.

The lady was standing outside the glass-paned front door looking inquisitively about her. She had on a most interesting hat, Harriet noticed, flowerpot-shaped and made of reddish furry material; out from under its brim curled green-and-white tendrils of Wandering Jew which then turned round and climbed up the sides of the hat. The lady's pale, smiling eyes peered from underneath this in rather an odd way.

"Well, little girl," the lady said, and Harriet took an instant dislike to her, "is your mummy in?"

"She doesn't live here," Harriet said politely, "this is my grandmother's house."

"I *see*," the lady said. "Well, may I see her then?" She spoke with a hint of impatience.

"I'm afraid everyone is out except me."

"*Oh*, dear," said the lady smiling, "then I shall have to explain to you. You see, the fact is that I am Miss Eaves, Wildrose Eaves, and I have been looking everywhere, but *every*where, for a quince tree. Well! I was driving along this lane and I looked up, and I said to myself, 'There's my quince tree!' so I came straight up here to ask if I could buy it."

"Do you mean," said Harriet doubtfully, "buy Granny's quince tree? Or do you want to buy some quinces? Because I don't think they'll be ripe for a few days, but we could let you know when we pick them."

"No, dear," said Miss Eaves patiently, "I want to buy the *tree*."

"I'm sure Granny would never think of selling the whole tree," said Harriet decidedly. "For one thing, wouldn't it die? And she's very very fond of it, I know—"

"I can see you don't quite understand, dear. I am Wildrose Eaves, *the* Wildrose Eaves, you know."

Harriet plainly didn't know, so the lady explained that she wrote a very famous article, which appeared in a Sunday paper every week, about gardening. "And people all over the world, you see, know every inch and corner of my mossy old garden just from reading about it in the *Sunday Tidings*."

"How nice," Harriet said.

"Well it *would* have been nice, dear, if there *was* such a garden, but the fact is the whole thing was made up. But now I've had this very tempting offer from an American magazine who want to come and take pictures of it, so you see I'm quickly putting the whole thing together, my charming old cottage, Shadie Thatch, and the yew hedges and pansy beds, but the one thing I couldn't get hold of was a quince tree, and that's very important because I've mentioned it more than once."

"Couldn't you say it had died?"

"Oh no, dear. Nothing in the garden at Shadie Thatch ever dies."

"Well," said Harriet, "I'm afraid it's not at all likely that Granny will want to sell the tree, but I'll tell her about it. Perhaps you could ring her up about tea-time?"

"Tell her I'll pay her five hundred pounds for the tree — with its quinces on naturally. That's most important," said the lady, and she ran down the steps again to her shiny car.

"I never heard such nonsense," said Granny when she came home and Harriet had made her put on her hearing-aid and pay attention to the matter. "Sell the quince tree! Whatever next? The woman's a fool, and about as shady as her thatch from the sound of her."

When the telephone rang she stamped off to give Miss Eaves a piece of her mind. Harriet heard her shouting, "I wouldn't take five hundred pounds nor yet five thousand. And that's my last word; no, certainly not, I shouldn't dream of it." And she rang off vigorously.

"Why," she went on, coming back and picking up her knitting, "your grandfather planted that tree the year we were married, and I've made quince jam from it for the last fifty years. The impertinence of her! But it's all the same nowadays – people think they can have all the benefits without doing any work for them."

And then it was time for supper and shortly after that time for Harriet and Mark to go to bed.

The children generally woke early in the mornings, and if it was fine they got up, took biscuits from the pantry, and went out riding. There were two fat, lazy ponies called Dapple and Grey who lived in the paddock at the bottom of the orchard and whose job it was to pull the roller over Granny's wide lawns, wearing felt slippers on their little feet. The children were allowed to ride them and although they could seldom be persuaded out of a jiggling trot it was a nice thing to do before breakfast. So next morning Harriet and Mark put on their jeans, went down through the orchard, caught the ponies with a bait of sugar, and took them up across the lawn to a side gate leading into the lane.

"We could go to Cloud Bottom," Mark was saying as they came round the corner of the house, "we haven't— good heavens, look!"

They both stared in astonishment and horror. For where, yesterday, the quince tree had grown, beautiful with its rusty leaves and golden fruit, this morning there was nothing but a huge, trampled, earthy hole.

"Tyre marks," said Mark, "and big ones. Someone's been here with a lorry or a big van."

"The beasts!" exclaimed Harriet. "That beastly woman! I thought she looked sly. Now what are we going to do?"

"I wonder how long they've been gone?"

"Granny'll be most dreadfully upset when she finds out."

"It's still jolly early," said Mark, looking at his watch, "and they can't have dug it up in the dark. I bet they haven't gone far yet. Let's follow the tracks and see if we can find which way they went. Do you remember where the woman said she lived?"

"Didn't give an address," Harriet said gloomily.

They mounted and went out into the lane. It was easy to see from the tyre marks and broken bushes where the lorry had backed in, and a trail of snapped twigs showed which way it had gone. Luckily the lane was a muddy one and when it widened the tread marks showed plainly. The children kicked Dapple and Grey into a sort of amble, their fastest gait, and went on like bloodhounds. They hadn't much idea what they would do if they caught up with the thieves, but they did feel very strongly that the tree must be put back before Granny discovered its loss.

"Remember the time when the black-marketeers stole the holly from the two round bushes? She was quite ill. Goodness knows what this would do to her."

"And the time when the little pippin tree died," Harriet said, nodding. "I say, look over there!"

The lane curved round a couple of meadows here, and

across the tops of three hedges they could see what looked like a big removal van, stationary at the edge of a little wood.

"I bet it's them," said Mark. "We must make a plan."

They cut across the fields, skirted the wood, and came out into the lane on the far side of the van. Here there were no tyre marks. "It's them all right," pronounced Mark. "We'd better send the ponies home – they may have seen them when they were taking the tree."

They dismounted and thumped off Dapple and Grey across the fields in the direction of home.

"Now you must limp," Mark said.

Harriet picked out two or three good sharp flints from the mud of the lane and put them in her shoes. She never did things by halves. Then they went on towards the van, which was still standing still. They saw two men sitting on the road bank, smoking.

The children walked slowly towards them, Harriet hobbling and clutching Mark's elbow.

"Up early, aren't you?" said one of the men. "What's the matter? Little girl hurt her foot?"

"I think I've sprained it," gasped Harriet.

"Could you possibly give us a lift?" said Mark. "I don't think she ought to walk on it."

"Where do you live?" asked one of the men.

"Lower Little Finching," answered Mark, inventing quickly.

"Never heard of it. We're going to Gorsham."

"Oh that would be fine. You could put us off at Gorsham crossroads."

The men finished their cigarettes and stood up, moving slowly towards the van. It was the usual enormously high furniture removal van, and said simply SMITH'S REMOVALS AND STORAGE on its side. Mark noticed with suppressed excitement that a couple of rusty leaves were jammed at the bottom of the roll-down steel back. He wanted to draw Harriet's attention to this but didn't dare.

"Lift the little girl in, Weaver," said the shorter man. "I want to check the fuel."

When he started he said, "First garage we see I must stop for juice. Only half a gallon left. All that winching used a lot."

The other man scowled at him in a silencing way. So they've got a winch inside there, thought Mark, run by a belt-drive off the engine. He had been wondering how they got the tree out of the ground and into the van.

The driver edged his way cautiously along the narrow track, which was called Back Lane because it swung out in a semicircle behind the village and then joined the main road again father along. Just past this road junction was Smalldown Garage and Ken Clement, who owned it, was a friend; it was Ken who came and mowed Granny's lawn with her crazy, temperamental old motor mower.

"I'll pull in here," said the driver when he saw Ken's sign.

"How about a bit of breakfast?" suggested Weaver, noticing that it also said Snacks.

"Okay. You want any breakfast, kids?"

"No thank you," said Mark, who was afraid that Ken would ruin things by greeting them. "We've had ours." He wished it were true.

"Well we shan't be long. You can stay in the cab if you want."

Both men jumped out and the driver called to Ken, who was hosing down a van, and asked him to fill up the tank. Then they went in at the café door which was round the side of the garage, out of sight.

"Now," said Mark to Harriet, "you must go in and distract their attention. Make a noise, play tunes on the juke-box or something, and don't forget to limp."

Harriet hobbled off. Her foot was really sore by now, she didn't have to pretend. In the café a fat girl was just giving the men plates of bacon and eggs. Luckily Harriet did not know her.

Harriet bought some chocolate and then limped across and put sixpence into the juke-box which jerked and rumbled once or twice and began to play a rather gloomy song:

> *"If she bain't a pal to me*
> *What care I whose pal she be?"*

"Oh blimey!" said Weaver. "I never can hear this song without crying."

"Why?" asked the other man.

"It reminds me so of the missus."

"Well, she's at home waiting for yer, isn't she?"

"Yes, that's just what I mean!" Sure enough, his face was all creased sideways, like a cracker that is just going to be pulled, and as the song went on its gloomy way he fairly burst out boo-hooing.

"Here, shall I turn the perishing thing off?"

"Oh no, Fred, don't do that. It's lovely – makes me feel ever so sad. Put in another sixpence and let's have it again. You don't hear it often nowadays."

"Lumme," said Fred, "there's no accounting for tastes." But he kindly put in another sixpence and started the tune again when it ended, while Weaver sat happily crying into his eggs.

Harriet went quietly out.

"It's all right," she said to Mark, who was waiting round in front. "They're good for another twenty minutes."

"That should do us; come on quick, Ken's waiting. He filled the tank and we had a good look inside (lucky thing that twig stuck out, it stopped the lock from engaging properly) and it's our tree all right."

They ran. Ken was in the driving cab already and his son Laurie was in the back; Harriet and Mark piled in with him. As Ken pulled out, his other son Tom ran a tractor across the drive-in with a deafening roar that effectively drowned the noise of their own departure.

It seemed queer to be riding along in a van with a quince tree. A few of the quinces had fallen off, but not so many as might have been expected.

"Must be a very well sprung van," Mark said.

"Proper shame, though, to take your Granny's quince tree like that," Laurie said. "Why not give those men in charge?"

"Oh, I expect they were just hired to do the job. The main thing is to get it back before Granny notices."

"Ar," Laurie said, "it's going to be a rare old fetch-me-round getting her out and back in the ground. Lucky there's this here crane on board."

They could feel the bumpy, slower progress as Ken edged the van up the lane, and the occasional swish of a branch against the sides. Then he stopped, turned, and backed into Granny's orchard gate.

Laurie stood up and prepared to jump out. "Cor," he said, "a blooming pusscat. Where did she come from?"

They all noticed the cat for the first time. She was sitting in the quince tree looking at them somewhat balefully-a big tortoiseshell with pale green eyes. Harriet was rather upset to notice also that the red flowerpot hat which had so much attracted her attention to Miss Eaves's head was lying at the foot of the tree.

"Do you think it's her?" she said apprehensively. "Miss Eaves? Now I come to think of it she did look as if she might be a witch."

"If so, why go to the trouble of hiring a van to steal the tree?"

"She couldn't take it across running water."

"That's true," Mark said. "Well, to be on the safe side we'd better stow her somewhere out of harm's way."

"I'll take her." Harriet clasped the cat firmly round its middle and tucked the red hat under her arm. Then she blushed, thinking how unsuitable this treatment was for the dignified Miss Eaves. If it was Miss Eaves.

"Still, it was jolly mean to steal Granny's tree," she said to the cat.

There were lots of unfurnished rooms at the back of Granny's house: apple rooms, onion rooms, tomato rooms, herb rooms and chutney rooms. Harriet shoved the reluctant cat into an apple room with a saucer of water, shut the door and window carefully, and raced back to the others. There was no one stirring in the house. It was still very early.

Ken had backed the van right up to the edge of the hole, and they had pulled down a ramp and were now swinging out a movable crane attached to one of the inside walls. The crane's padded clutch was still holding on to the quince tree's trunk which was all wrapped in felt for protection. Ken got back into the cab and started the engine, and the crane cable tightened and began to throb. The quince tree lurched slightly.

Ken jumped out again. "You kids get in the back there and push," he said. "Laurie, pass this rope round the tree and swing her if she goes skew. I'll work the crane."

Little by little the tree slid forward along the polished steel floor of the van and began to slither down the ramp. The roots, which had been pressed up against the walls, sprang out straight.

"Handy little gadget that crane is, in a furniture van," Laurie said, giving the rope a tug and wiping his face with an earthy hand. "Now we're going to have fun, though, getting her back in the hole."

It wasn't so bad as he feared — the hole was far larger than the tree needed and it was just a case of tumping it up and down to make sure the roots were all comfortable. Then, working like beavers, they piled the earth back into the hole and trampled it down.

"It looks terrible," Harriet said. "As if wild bulls had been here."

"Turf, that's what we want," said Laurie. "This here grass'll take a month of Sundays to come back."

"Turf down by the cricket pavilion," said his father. "We was just going to renew the pitch. The club won't begrudge old Mrs Armitage half a load."

They swung the crane inboard again, hauled down the back (Mark jammed a twig in at the bottom, just as it had been before) and all piled into the cab. Ken hustled the van back down the lane to the garage.

Tom was still exercising his tractor in the drive-in. He gave them a reassuring wave. "Haven't come out yet," he shouted.

Sure enough, when Harriet tiptoed to the café window and peered in the two van men were still drinking tea, and Weaver was crying while he listened to a tune that went:

"*Oh, breathe not her name, or don't breathe it often.*"

She often wondered how long it was before they discovered that the tree had gone.

Meanwhile Ken had collected a load of turf from the cricket pitch and took it back in the tractor-trailer. They all helped pack the turfs round the foot of the quince tree, working outwards until they met the unspoilt grass.

"Lucky it was lawn underneath," Ken said, "and not rose-garden or summit. That wouldn't have been so easy to fake. Now you fetch the ponies and we'll give the turf a good old flattening."

"We'd better have the quinces picked as quickly as possible," Harriet remarked as they laced on the ponies' felt shoes and harnessed them to the roller, "in case Miss Eaves has another try. Once the quinces are off, the tree isn't any use to her."

"I noticed the telephone linesmen as we were coming through the village from the pavilion," Mark said, "I'll ask them to come and help."

The linesmen always helped Granny pick her fruit, and when they heard Mark's story they said they would be along with their ladders right away. Ken said he supposed he had better go back and look after the business, and he drove off, waving aside the thanks of Mark and Harriet.

"Never thought she'd look so good," he shouted. The ponies were shuffling round and round with the roller and the grass beneath the tree had begun to look as if it had been there all its life. A few leaves and one more quince had fallen.

"Well, us'll make a start," said the leader of the telephone men.

"I'll just go and tell Granny you're here," said Harriet. "It's ten minutes to breakfast-time."

Granny was delighted to hear that the men had begun on the quinces; she said ever since that woman had called she had been thinking about quince chutney. As soon as breakfast was over, without even going out to look at the tree, she got out a cookery book and a cauldron, told Nursie to make some strong tea with molasses in it for the men, and instructed the children to bring in all the quinces that had been picked.

Soon the house was full of the aromatic scent of Granny's quince, tomato and onion chutney, and Mark and Harriet were kept busy peeling, chopping, and running to and fro with more supplies, while old Nursie doddered around ordering everybody about and taking the men enormous jam tarts.

"Do you think the tree will be all right?" Harriet said to Mark as they stood watching the last of the quinces come down.

"Oh, I should think so," he said. "That's that, now we can let Miss Eaves out. If it is Miss Eaves."

Harriet ran indoors with the last basketful.

"Put them in the quince room, child," said Granny, stirring away at her pungent brew. "And then come back and have a good sniff at this steam; it will cure your cough. By the way—"

"Oh!" exclaimed Harriet, stopping on the kitchen hearth. "How did *she* get here?"

"I was going to ask you that," said Granny mildly. "I heard her mewing in the apple room. She's not one of the village cats."

Miss Eaves was sitting comfortably on the hearthstone, washing her tortoiseshell paw with a pink tongue. If it was Miss Eaves. How had she mewed loud enough to penetrate Granny's deafness, Harriet wondered.

"I've been wanting a cat," Granny went on. "Ever since old Opussum went to sleep in the laurel tree the mice have been getting at the codlins. So I buttered her paws and I shall keep her – unless, of course, anyone turns up to claim her."

Harriet was rather taken aback, but Miss Eaves looked uncommonly placid and pleased with herself. An empty sardine saucer stood at one side of the hearth.

After she had had her good sniff at the quince steam (which did indeed cure her cough) Harriet ran off to consult with Mark.

"If she's had her paws buttered," he said gloomily, "she'll probably never leave of her own accord. We shall have our work cut out to get rid of her."

And certainly a tactful taking of Miss Eaves to the boundary hedge and dropping her over it did nothing to dislodge her; there were so many windows kept open in Granny's house that she could always get in one or another of them and turn up purring in time for the next meal.

Meanwhile, to the children's relief, the quince tree showed no signs of ill effects from its upheaval.

On Nursie's next W.I. afternoon Granny was making quince honey in the kitchen when Harriet saw the Brushitoff Brush man drive up to the door.

"Do you want any brushes today, Granny?" she shouted through the steam. "The brush man's here."

"No, child. Last week we had an onion brush, the week before a tomato brush, and the week before that a tin of apple polish. Nothing this week, tell him, thank you."

On the way to the front door Harriet found Mark and hissed her plan to him, also borrowing all the money he had, which was sevenpence.

"Granny doesn't want anything, thank you," she said to the man, "But may I look at what you've got? I want to buy a — a present."

The Brushitoff man rapidly undid his suitcase and spread out a most multifarious display of brushes — straight, curved, circular, pliable, stiff, nylon, bristle, sponge, and all colours of the rainbow.

"Oh, how lovely," Harriet said admiringly. "Gracious, isn't it hard to decide. How much is that one?"

"Three and sixpence, madam."

"And this?"

"Five and eleven."

"Oh dear, they do cost a lot, don't they? How much is this little one?"

"Two and six."

Harriet went on hopefully digging in the suitcase. She tried out a muff-brush on her cuff and a pot-plant swab on her fingertip. Finally, after much thought, she purchased a tiny button-brush that cost only a shilling. The man collected all the brushes together and drove off in his van.

"Well," said Harriet, meeting Mark breathless on the path outside, "did you do it?"

Mark nodded. "Took Miss Eaves round out the back door and popped her in the van."

"Loose?"

"No, I put her in an empty apple-polish carton. She'll get out in half an hour or so."

"That should be enough," said Harriet, satisfied.

They hoped they had heard the last of Miss Eaves.

Next morning though, at breakfast, Granny sat looking very puzzled over a letter on lavender-coloured writing paper on which the printed heading Wildrose Eaves nestled among a cluster of forget-me-nots.

"Most extraordinary," said Granny suspiciously, "here's some woman writing to thank me for her delightful visit when to the best of my knowledge she's never been near the place. Says how much she's looking forward to another visit. Must be mad – isn't Eaves the name of the person who wanted my quince tree?"

In fact it soon appeared that Miss Eaves found catching mice in Granny's apple rooms much more to her taste than writing untruthful gardening articles for the *Sunday Tidings*. After three days she was back again, purring beside the kitchen stove, and the children gave up trying to persuade her to go away. Though Harriet never really became accustomed to waking up and finding a lady journalist who was also a witch sleeping on the end of her bed.

"Dear me," Granny said, some weeks after the children had gone back to school, "there must have been a gale one night recently. That quince tree has blown completely round. The big branch used to be on the south side. And I never heard a thing, not a thing. Just fancy that, puss."

But Miss Eaves, purring round her ankles, said nothing, and Granny strolled on to look at the medlar tree, murmuring, "I'm getting very old; very, very old, puss; very, very old."

Seven

SMOKE FROM CROMWELL'S TIME

THERE WAS THIS young man, Danny Monk, a wheelwright and carpenter by trade, who got a legacy from his auntie in Australia. Well, some folk advised he should do one thing with the money, and some another, but Dan himself had no doubts on the matter.

"I've always fancied the antique business," he said, "and now's my chance." So he began looking about for a little shop that would suit him, and presently found one in the town of Kingbury, about six miles from his own village. It had been a sweetshop before, until the old lady who ran it decided to retire and live with her married son, so for three days Dan had to leave the doors and windows open, for he couldn't abide the smell of mouldy liquorice in the place, not to speak of wet, mildewy peppermints; meanwhile he was busy as a bee scrubbing the floor (ankle-deep in toffee-papers), washing and painting the sticky walls a beautiful speedwell blue, fitting new glass panes in the door and window (the old ones were so scratched that even the sun through them looked like a Queen Victoria farthing) and hanging a fine sign which said: *D. Monk, Old Junk.*

Well, when you move as far as six miles away from home there's things about the new part you don't always know, and Danny did wonder why he got some odd glances and some knowing looks from people as they strolled up and down the hill, keeping an eye on all he was doing to his new premises. Wonderful lot of spare time folk in Kingbury did seem to have. But perfectly pleasant and civil they were, to be sure, admiring all he did. Every now and then, in between jobs, he wondered, too, why the place had been going so cheap, but that was just his luck, he reckoned; he had always known he was a lucky one, ever since the church clock in his home village fell down, just missing him, and burying itself so deep in the ground that the Parish Council have left it there to this day, with naught but five to twelve showing above the cobbles.

Soon as Dan had the place tidied up to his satisfaction, out he went, scouring round the country in an old pony-trap he'd bought, attending all the auctions and sales, picking up here a pot and there a settle, here an old antique pair of fire-dogs and there a bundle of curtains and tapestry, till he had his shop nicely filled.

One morning soon after that an old lady came in.

"Morning, ma'am," said Dan, running a hand through his black hair to tidy it. "What can I do for you?"

"Just having a look round," said she. "What's this, then?"

"That's Hereward the Wake's breadboard," said he, for he'd been careful to find out the history of everything he bought.

"Ah. What about this?"

"Queen Matilda's nutcrackers."

"Indeed. And this?"

"That's King John's bundle that got lost in the Wash."

"How about this?"

"Genuine palm-leaf fly-swatter brought back from the crusades. And that's the suit of armour that goes with it."

"What about this alarm-clock?"

"Ethelred the Unready left it on Watling Street."

"I see," she said. "And this old chest?"

"Heirloom of the Pym family. Last survivor sold it to me," said Dan.

"Why's the bottom drawer nailed up?"

"Because that bottom drawer, ma'am, is still full of gunsmoke from Cromwell's time, from the Great Civil War!"

"Fancy!" said the old lady. "Nice lot of stuff you've got together, I won't deny."

"Looks a bit better in here than it did last week this time, doesn't it?" said Danny.

"That's so," said the old lady, laughing very hearty. Then she told him that she was the previous owner, Mrs Friendly.

Dan was a bit abashed at that, fearing he might have hurt her feelings.

"No offence, my boy, no offence at all," said she. "Very nicely you've done it up. I just dropped in to tell you so, and to mention about the apanage and appurtenances."

"Appurtenances? What's that?" said Dan.

"Maybe the house agents didn't tell you?" said the old lady, sitting down and making herself comfortable on King John's washing. "Whoever lives here takes on the job of town witch as well. Or wizard, as the case may be."

"I'm no witch!" said Danny, rather put out.

"Oh, you'll learn, you'll learn," said Mrs Friendly. "You look a clever lad enough. And I don't mind coming to give you a bit of advice from time to time. Staying up the hill at the Six Bells, I am now, with my son."

Well, Danny saw there was no help for it, so he was quite glad to have Mrs Friendly's advice when people came asking for love-potions or end-games, charms against toothache or remedies for the sheep-shrink. And she soon formed the habit of dropping in of an evening for a chat, finding him sociably inclined and always ready to take instruction (besides, they had a noisy lot of customers up at the Six Bells, for ever singing and thumping on the bar).

Dan soon picked up a fair amount of information about the town from Mrs Friendly.

"There's a thing that puzzles me, ma'am," he said to her one evening. "When the customers from the Six Bells come out at closing time, you can hear them singing all sorts of different songs outside the pub. But, time they get down here, past the shop, they all seem to be singing the same words – Bunches of Roses, Bunches of Roses, over and over again. Why's that?"

"They're asleep," said Mrs Friendly. "Hadn't you noticed? They fall asleep when they come abreast of this cottage, and go sleep-walking down the hill."

"What's the reason for that, then, ma'am?"

"Why, you see," she said, "there's a time-fault just halfway down the hill, where this cottage stands."

"A time-fault, ma'am?"

"You've heard of a geological fault?" said Mrs Friendly. "When one bit of the ground slips away from another, so that you're liable to get earthquakes? Well, a time-fault's the same thing, only with time; one bit slips away from another."

"Eh?" said Danny.

"Haven't you noticed a kind of a tingle, like an electric shock, when you walk by? If you've a drop of beer inside you, it puts you to sleep. And sometimes it puts you right back into another part of time – or forward, of course, depending which way you're going. Sometimes a loud noise, say a clap of thunder, will set it off."

"Bit awkward, that," said Dan.

"Oh, it doesn't happen very often. There was a sad case of it once," said Mrs Friendly, settling herself down more snugly on King John's underpinnings.

"When was that, then, ma'am?"

"Time of the Danes," said Mrs Friendly. "There was one of them turned up, with his men and his ships from the north. Landed over at Danestrand and came along here, turned all the monks out of the monastery, which, he said, would do for his palace, and made himself king of the district. Ragnar Bushybeard, he was called, and not a bad king, so I've heard, apart from turning out the monks."

"Where did they go?"

"Built themselves a new monastery out on the marshes. They weren't fussy; all *they* wanted to do was heal the sick and make rose-petal cordial. Wonderful district for roses it is here, as you'll have noticed."

True enough, the whole town of Kingbury was smothered in climbing roses, summertimes, and all the hedges on the marsh were full of sweetbriar; you could smell their sweetness as far as ten miles out to sea.

"So what happened?"

"Time went by," said Mrs Friendly. "People got used to King Ragnar and he married a local woman, Mary Binnamoor, and they had a daughter."

"What was *her* name?"

"Freylinde. Princess Freylinde. Mad about horses, she was, like most girls, and she had a colt called Goldenhope which could gallop faster than any other in the district."

"That's funny," said Dan. "the old cob I bought is called Goldenhope."

"Lots of nags round here have had that name ever since," Mrs Friendly said.

"And so? What happened next?"

"More time went by and another lot of Danes came plundering down from the north. Outlandish lot of blaggards, those Danes," said Mrs Friendly. "Fight each other as soon as anybody else. They told King Ragnar – who was their own cousin – that he'd got to pay them tax or else they'd break up the town."

"Did he pay them?"

"Not he! Made them a sporting offer, instead. He said he'd pay them if they could produce a horse that would outrun his, racing three times round the city walls. Otherwise they were to leave the place in peace. All those Danes were mad keen on sport, so they agreed, and sailed off home, promising to be back in a year with the fastest horse in Denmark."

"Princess Freylinde would be riding Goldenhope against their horse?"

"That was the plan. But you can guess what happened."

"No," Dan said anxiously. "No, I can't guess."

"One day Princess Freylinde was walking down the hill, just hereabouts. Of course the town was a bit different in those times. Walking down the hill, she was, going to give her pony a bit o' sugar and a handful of roses – roses are wonderful good for a horse's coat, *and* for its wind, they say – slipped – fell into the time-fault – and vanished clean away. Nothing left of her but the bunch of roses."

"Oh dear," said Dan.

"You may well say oh dear. King Ragnar nearly went distracted. (His wife had died the year before.) First he blamed the monks; thought they'd kidnapped the princess out of revenge for having their monastery taken. That was on account of the bunch of roses left lying in the street; he thought the monks had left them as a sign. So he burned down their new monastery and turned them out all over again. But that didn't bring Freylinde back. There was a song made up at that time:

"He has lost the girl with the golden hair
His beautiful daughter so radiant and rare,
He has called, he has hunted everywhere
But she isn't on land or sea or air;
All he can see wherever he goes is
Bunches of roses, bunches of roses,
Bunches of roses.

"He has lost his mistress, so kind and sweet
Who combed his mane and who washed his feet
Who brought him sugar and kibbled wheat
And other delectable things to eat;
All he can see wherever he goes is
Bunches of roses, bunches of roses,
Bunches of roses."

"Was it about the king or about the horse?"

"Both," said Mrs Friendly. "That's what you hear them

singing when they come past at night; the song's in the air hereabouts, as you might say."

"So what did the king do then?"

"Died of grief."

"Poor fellow."

"There was some said it served him right for turning the monks out of their monastery. Anyway, the townsfolk gave him a lovely funeral, and he lies up there, with his ship and his shield and a lot of gold pots and skillets, under the big, grassy Castle Mound at the top of the town."

"I always wondered what was under there," said Danny. "Go on. Did the Danes come back next year?"

"They did. Long before that, of course, everybody in the town was in a fair fret, wondering what to do when it came to the race. No king, no princess."

"They still had the horse?"

"Yes, but Goldenhope would only go fast for his mistress. Without her, he pined and dwindled, hardly touched a morsel of his feed, until his ribs stood out like buttresses and his poor eyes had sunk right back in his head. So there didn't seem much hope of his winning. But – you'll hardly believe it – just one week before the Danes were due to land, Princess Freylinde tumbled back out of wherever she'd got lodged in time."

"Good gracious," Dan said. "That was a bit of luck, then."

"Well, it was and it wasn't," said Mrs Friendly. "But who's this coming? Sounds as if you've got a customer."

A young, thin girl came bolting into the shop, panting as

if she'd used up all her day's ration of breath and was drawing on tomorrow's.

"Save me, save me!" she gasped; she seemed near distracted with fright.

"It's young Effie from up at the pub," said Mrs Friendly. "What's the matter, Effie, for goodness' sake?"

"Who's after you?" said Dan.

Then they heard a furious voice outside, shouting, "Stop that girl!"

The girl Effie had been holding a big green walnut leaf clutched in her fingers, and now she seemed to get back her wits a bit and, casting her eyes round the shop, she spied the big old black chest that was an heirloom of the Pym family and still held a bushel of New Model Army smoke; quick as a flash Effie slid the walnut leaf through the crack above the bottom drawer and poked it inside.

Next minute a big, brawny, black-eyed woman bounced into the shop.

"Give me that leaf, you little good-for-nothing!" she bawled, in a voice like a rusty barrel rolling over cobbles, and she made for Effie with an empty stout bottle.

"Why," said Mrs Friendly, "if it isn't my daughter-in-law! What's up, Flossie? Left poor Tom looking after the pub all on his own, have you?"

Young Mrs Thomas Friendly – she looked far from friendly just then, or ever, for the matter of that – made a grab at Effie, who ducked out of the way and got behind the crusader's armour.

"Where's my leaf, you little bag of bones?" And, snatching up the crusader's fly-swatter, Flossie aimed a blow at the girl.

"Here, missis," said Dan, who felt some account of all these goings-on was due to him, as owner of the premises. "What's all this about a leaf?"

"You'd better tell me where she put that leaf, my lad, or I'll sue!" Mrs Floss said, rounding on him.

"You've no right to the leaf. I picked it, and it's mine," said Effie.

"My walnut tree!" snapped Floss. "Leastways my husband's, which comes to the same."

"*You*'d never have climbed the tree, right up, and picked the tippermost leaf," said Effie. "Never! The branches would have broken before you was halfway up."

"Will one of you ladies kindly tell me what all this is about?" said Dan.

" 'Tis a wishing-tree, that walnut in the Six Bells yard," explained old Mrs Friendly. "Pick the topmost leaf, sleep with it next to your heart, and you get your heart's desire."

"Well, for heaven's sake! What's to stop the lass going back now for the next topmost leaf?"

"Ah, you can only do it once. Once every five years, that is."

"So you'd better hand over that walnut leaf, young man, and smartly," said Floss. "For it's plain she's hidden it somewhere about the shop."

And she began turning over bundles and looking under boxes.

"Matter of fact," said Dan, "neither of you can have the leaf without you pay me fifty pound, for that's the price of the chest. The drawer with the leaf in it is nailed up, see, and you can't open the drawer without letting out all that historical smoke, left over from Cromwell's time, and that I wouldn't do for the Queen of Sheba herself, not unless she was to put the cash down first. The chest's nothing like so valuable without the smoke."

Well, that fairly flummoxed them. Mrs Floss Friendly stormed and stamped, but Dan took no notice of her temper. "Fifty pound," he said, "or that leaf stays where it is."

"I'll work for you for a year for nothing," said Effie quietly. "I'll dust your stock and scrub your kitchen and cook your dinner and mind the shop while you're out, if you'll keep the chest and let me have the leaf at the end of the year."

That sounded like a fair offer: Dan had already found that he needed someone in the shop while he was out looking for goods. And furthermore he had taken a liking to the girl who, though so small and pale and scrawny, stood up to Mrs Floss as bold as a mother-mouse, once she had her breath back.

"I'm agreeable," he said. But Mrs Floss snapped:

"The girl works for me!"

"I'll be your skivvy no longer," said Effie. "I've stood as much as I'm going to of the pinches and thumps I get up at the Six Bells."

"That's the gratitude you get for taking in an orphanage brat!" said Floss.

But Effie had made her mind up, so she arranged with Dan that she should sleep in the loft over the stable beside the shop, and she went off directly to fetch her bundle.

That still didn't settle Mrs Floss, however: she threatened and raged, and said she would have the law on Dan.

"Can't we fix up the matter peaceful and neighbourly?" said he. Old Mrs Friendly, still sitting on King John's laundry, smiled to herself. "Tell me, missis," Dan went on, "What is this heart's desire of yours you're so set on? Maybe we could come at it some other way?" And he fished out the book of everyday, household spells which Mrs Friendly had passed on to him along with the goodwill of the business.

"I want to be more beautiful than any other female in this town!" said Mrs Floss.

Well, anybody could see that this was a tall order, for Mrs Floss was about the size and shape of a tar barrel, beetroot-coloured, with three warts sprouting black hairs on her chin. But Dan didn't seem too worried.

"Oh, if that's all I think we can manage it," he said, turning over the pages. "Yes, now, let's see; pinch of sulphur – lucky I laid some in for the moths in the tapestry; two blades of grass that's never been stepped on – I can get those from the front garden;" (for there was a little fenced-in patch out front where nobody ever set foot) "rose cordial as used by Helen of Troy – as it happens I've a bottle of the very stuff which I picked up yesterday over at Bury St Edmunds; pound all together in a mortar till it bubbles, and fan to cool with genuine Holy Land palm leaves. May I trouble you for that fly-swatter, ma'am?"

"I never did see a quicker hand at learning the business," old Mrs Friendly said, smiling still wider. And her daughter-in-law, quite soothed and softened, took the potion, which Danny handed her in a pewter pipkin, and swallowed it down. Straight away she turned into a peacock, and spread out her dazzling tail with a loud boastful squawk.

"*Out*side, if you don't mind, missis," Dan said, and gently shoved her through the front door on to the little patch of grass. There she (or rather he) sat preening his tail and admiring his reflection in the shop window.

"I had to make it a cock bird," Dan explained, "for the female peahen's only a little brown thing."

"Oh, don't apologize," said Mrs Friendly. "My son will be a happier man than since the day she dragged him to the altar. But I'd best get back and help him, for he'll be short-handed at the pub."

Effie settled in to the stable-loft and soon Dan began to wonder how he had ever managed without her help in the shop, for she kept it spick and span, besides being so civil and smiling to the customers that he just about doubled his trade. As well as that she baked him beautiful seed-cakes and treacle-tarts for his tea, gave nuts to the peacock, and planted a pair of rose bushes either side the front door which straightway put out handsome blooms, red on the left, white on the right. Moreover she fed and groomed the old cob, gave him tidbits of roseleaves and sugarknobs, brushed his mane, plaited his tail, and whispered in his ear, till he was the proudest pony in the district, and went bowling over the countryside with Dan as if he thought he'd been entered for the Gold Cup. And furthermore she herself, now she was not harassed and harried, pinched and thumped and thwacked and fed on nothing but leavings by Mrs Floss, began to fill out until she became as pretty as a sweetpea, with hair the colour of corn silk.

But in spite of the improvement in her looks she was not at all a flighty girl; she liked to go and sit, of an evening, up on the grassy Castle Mound, looking out over the water meadows beyond the town "trying to remember", as she told Dan, "where she had been born"; or, if Dan had not driven out that day, she would exercise the cob, cantering him along the towpath towards the sea, for like all girls, she was mad about horses.

Or she would study in old Mrs Friendly's book of spells, so as to help with the customers.

"How did you ever come to be working at the Six Bells?" Dan asked her one day, as they sat over their treacle-tart.

"Why, you see, when I was a bit smaller I was found wandering; couldn't remember my folks or my name; so I went to the orphanage (where they christened me Effie because I was found on a Friday). They don't keep you at the orphanage once you're over four foot high, so when I'd grown a bit I had to take the first job that offered. But I like it much better here than at the Six Bells."

"I should think so!" said Dan. "Though it's true the customers up there don't seem such a rowdy lot now Mrs Tom Friendly isn't there. But they still sing that song about Bunches of Roses."

This reminded him he'd never heard the end of the story about Princess Freylinde and the horse Goldenhope. It had slipped his mind, with all the excitement about the walnut leaf and the old Civil War chest; he tied a knot in his handkerchief so's he'd remember to ask old Mrs Friendly about it next time she came in. But she didn't have so much time to come calling nowadays, since she was giving her son Tom a lot of help up at the Six Bells; he having declared that, once out of the noose, he'd as soon not risk matrimony again.

Effie asked Dan if she could move the Civil War chest out to the loft so there would be no risk of it getting sold by mistake; also then, even if she could not take out her precious walnut leaf, at least she was near it at night and could sleep close by it, stretched out on her straw mattress, with the old bay cob whickering in his dreams underneath.

"You never said what *your* heart's desire was," he said, as they shifted the heavy, awkward thing up the loft stairs. "Maybe there'd be some easier way of getting it than working a whole year for one withered walnut leaf?"

"No, there wouldn't," said Effie. "I know I *have* a heart's desire, because I dream about it sometimes at night, and when I wake up my cheeks are wet with tears of longing for it. But what it is, I can never remember – only that it's something very far off and beautiful."

Poor Dan was a bit dashed at that, since he was growing uncommonly fond of the girl and would have been glad to give her a necklace of pearls or whatever in the wide world she fancied. In fact several times he offered to prise open the bottom drawer before the end of the year, but, no, she said, she'd made a bargain and she believed in sticking by a bargain fairly. And he had to respect her for that.

So time went by and the only trouble they had was with the peacock. For a start, Mrs Floss had never had a kindly nature; maybe she had found that being more beautiful than all the women in the town wasn't as satisfactory as she'd hoped; maybe she pined for cheerful old times behind the bar in the Six Bells; whatever the cause, the peacock grew more and more bad-tempered, squawking out its shrill unchancy cry all day long, as if trying to frighten away the customers from Dan's shop. And furthermore it became plain that the bird bore a grudge against Effie, as if it felt envy and spite on account of her improved looks; it began going for her, pecking, scratching, and downright vicious, when she carried out its morning and evening bowl of peanuts and rose petals, until Dan had to take over the feeding of it.

Well, one evening Dan was returning to the shop after attending an auction in a big house t'other side of the county; he'd bought a lot of stuff: pictures, books, chairs, and a silver rose-bowl that was said to have belonged once upon a time to Fair Rosamund. He came home late and slow, on account of his load, and he stopped at the Six Bells for a drink, since he was dry from all the dusty old books he'd leafed through.

Old Mrs Friendly was in the bar, neat and sedate as a downy owl.

"Well there, Dan," she said. "Trade all right?"

"Champion," said Dan. Then the knot in his handkerchief reminded him, and he said:

"While I'm here, Mrs Friendly, you never did tell me the end of that story."

"Which story would that be?" she said. "About the swan in the Town Hall cafeteria? Or the furnished room they found on the rubbish dump? Or the old Romans who thought they could stop the spring coming? Or the merman that got landed high and dry after the great storm of 1588?"

"No, none of those," he said, "but about Princess Freylinde and the horse Goldenhope. What happened when she came back? Did she win the race against the Danes?"

"Ah," said Mrs Friendly, "there's different opinions about the end of that story. You know how it is with history – the books don't agree. One tale has it that she got back to find her poor pony so thin and weak from grieving that he could hardly hobble to the starting-line. But he brightened up wonderfully at sight of her and let out a whinny that could be heard as far away as Orford Ness. So she gave him a feed of corn simmered in wine and rode him out. Well, when the Danes laid eyes on the poor nag that was to run against the champion racer of all Denmark, they laughed so much they nearly choked on their beards. Just the same, the townspeople had the last laugh. For Goldenhope, thin and weak as he was, went like the wind out of joy to have his mistress back, and passed the finishing post a whole round of the town ahead of the Danish horse. But that was the end of him, for he dropped dead as he passed the post, and they buried him on the spot; folk say that if you look at the town wall, just near the Strand Gate, you can see a little carving of a horse that's nearly worn away with wind and weather."

"Oh, poor Goldenhope," said Dan sadly. "And poor Freylinde. I wonder what she did then?"

"Well, there's some say she wouldn't race her tired horse at all, but instead, offered to marry the Danish king if he'd leave the town in peace. And there's others say she did race, and did win, but it was a different horse. Certain anyway it is that she was queen for many years after that, and there's a lock of her golden hair woven into the bishop's embroidered mantle that he wears on feast days. And a lock of her husband's hair too."

"Her husband?" said Dan. "What—"

But just as he began to ask his question he was interrupted by the most fearsome screaming down the hill; it sounded as if all the pigs in the world were having their tails twisted.

"The peacock!" Mrs Friendly exclaimed. "What mischief is that fowl up to now?"

She and Dan rushed outside, followed by all the other customers in the pub. And, down the hill, outside the junk shop, they saw the peacock, fanning its tail, darting its beak, flashing its furious head, and all the while letting out this mad piercing scream at Effie, who was taking it a bowl of peanuts and rose petals.

"Effie!" shouted Dan. "Wait for me! I'll feed it!"

But he spoke too late.

Then he saw the strangest sight that ever he'd seen in all his life – saw the air down the hill give a kind of shudder and slip sideways, the way you will see a mirage trickle together like a pool of water across the road on a hot day; and he saw young Effie, with her bowl of peanuts and rose petals – saw her one minute and not the next, for she slipped into a fold of the clear air and vanished from view. And was gone!

"Eh, dear," said Mrs Friendly. "I should have thought o' that. It was the peacock screaming that set it off, I daresay."

"Peacock screaming? What do you mean?"

"Like the sound of a trumpet will break a glass, sometimes. That fowl's ill-omened voice has opened up the time-fault and the lass has fallen through."

"You mean she's gone?" said Dan, all distracted. "You mean she won't come back?"

He ran down the hill to the front of his shop. Nothing to be seen there but the peacock, crazily folding and unfolding its tail, and a scatter of peanuts and rose petals across the flagstones.

Mrs Friendly came along down and looked about. "Yes, that's what's happened," she said. "Let's hope she's got back to where she came from."

"Came from?"

"I always suspicioned that was how she arrived in the first place."

"But how can we find out where she's gone?"

"That's a hard one," said Mrs Friendly. "And the answer is, I don't know."

Dan sat down on the front step of his shop, fairly winded by the blow.

"I was going to ask her to marry me," he said brokenly. "At the end of the year, when she'd got her heart's desire."

"Maybe she has her heart's desire already," said Mrs Friendly. "Maybe her heart's desire was to be back home again. That'd be a fine joke on Floss here." And she gave the peacock a thump with the pewter mug she was carrying. "Anyway, no use to grieve too much, lad, there's not a thing in the world you can do."

Off she went, back to the Six Bells.

Dan slowly gathered up all the scattered rose petals (he left the peanuts for the peacock) and went into his silent, neat shop.

He went through to the loft and he looked at her tidy little straw mattress, her brush and comb laid together on the sill, and the Civil War chest, with its bottom drawer nailed shut. Inside that drawer, along with a lot of New Model smoke, was the heart's desire leaf.

"It's her leaf, not mine," said Dan. "Hers, all but six weeks. I've no right to touch it."

He went back to the Six Bells to fetch Goldenhope, who

was still patiently waiting outside the taproom door, his head hanging between the shafts of the trap.

For two days Dan seemed like a dazed man. He sold a walrus tooth, property of Leif Eriksson, for tenpence, and the leash of Prince Rupert's dog Boy for half a crown. He hardly spoke, but sometimes people heard him singing:

> "*He has lost the girl who helped in the store,*
> *He misses her daily more and more,*
> *His heart is heavy, his heart is sore,*
> *He feels like an apple without a core.*
> *All he can see, wherever he goes is*
> *Bunches of roses, bunches of roses,*
> *Bunches of roses.*"

Then, on the third night, as he lay tossing and turning, he thought he had a dream. He thought he dreamed that Effie came to him and laid her hand on his, gentle as a feather.

"Dan!" she whispered. "Danny! Be a good friend to me! Lend me Goldenhope?"

"Yes, all right," he muttered in his dream. "The stable key's on the nail."

A moment later she was gone and he almost went back to sleep. Yet a moment later than *that*, he could have sworn he heard the clatter of hooves. *Had* it been a dream?

Suddenly he leapt out of bed like a madman, pulled on his trousers, and raced downstairs, out through the shop door. For now he could hear the hooves clattering in the street outside, and the peacock stirring, letting out a surly croak in its sleep, from under its wing.

"Wait!" Dan cried. "Wait, Effie, wait! Take me along too."

And that was the last that was heard of Danny Monk. Next morning, neither speck nor hair was to be seen, of him or his cob; only the peacock sulked, flashing, on the little front patch of grass.

Some folk were surprised, but not Mrs Friendly.

"Ah," she said. "That was a clever lass. I thought she'd find her way home sooner or later, but I didn't guess she'd have the wit to take Danny with her. I ought to have guessed, though, that all her study of my book would be some use to her. For isn't the golden lock in the bishop's mantle plaited along with another one that's black? And whoever heard of a black-haired Dane?"

Mrs Friendly's son took on a potman to help him, and she moved back to the junk shop. Somebody had to run it, after all.

She still has the Civil War Chest in the loft, with its nailed-up drawer full of smoke and its heart's-desire leaf. But the chest is not for sale.

"After all," she tells the customers, "they may come back for it some day."

Eight

THE APPLE OF TROUBLE

IT WAS A black day for the Armitage family when Great-Uncle Gavin retired. In fact, as Mark pointed out, Uncle Gavin did not exactly retire; he was pushed. He had been High Commissioner of Mbutam-Mbutaland, which had suddenly decided it needed a High Commissioner no longer, but would instead become the Republic of Mbutambuta. So Sir Gavin Armitage, K.C.M.G., O.B.E., D.S.O., and so forth, was suddenly turned loose on the world, and because he had expected to continue living at the High Commissioner's Residence for years to come and had no home of his own, he moved in with the parents of Mark and Harriet.

The first disadvantage was that he had to sleep in the ghost's room. Mr Peake was nice about it, he said he quite understood, and they would probably shake down together very well, he had been used to all sorts of odd company in his three hundred years. But after a few weeks of Great-Uncle Gavin's keep-fit exercises, coughing, thumping, harrumphing, snoring, and blazing open windows, Mr Peake became quite thin and pale (for a ghost); he migrated through the wall into the room next door, explaining apologetically that he wasn't getting a wink of sleep. Unfortunately the room next door was a bathroom, and Mr Armitage complained that it gave him the jumps to see a ghostly face suddenly loom up beside his in the mirror when he was shaving. Great-Uncle Gavin never noticed Mr Peake at all. He was not sensitive. Besides he had other things to think about.

One of his main topics of conversation was how disgracefully the children had been brought up. He was horrified at the way they were allowed to live all over the house, instead of being pent in some upstairs nursery.

"Little gels should be seen and not heard," he boomed at Harriet whenever she opened her mouth. To get her out from underfoot during the holidays he insisted on her enrolling in a domestic science course run by a Professor Grimalkin who had recently come to live in the village.

As for Mark, he had hardly a minute's peace.

"God bless my soul, boy –" nearly all Great-Uncle Gavin's remarks began with this request – "God bless my soul, what are you doing now? *Reading?* God bless my soul, do you want to grow up a muff?"

"A muff, Great-Uncle? What is a muff, exactly?" And Mark pulled out the notebook in which he was keeping a glossary of Great-Uncle Gavin.

"A muff, why, a muff is a – a funk, sir, a duffer, a frowst, a tug, a swot, a miserable little sneaking *milksop*!"

Mark was so busy writing down all these words that he forgot to be annoyed.

"You ought to be out of doors, sir, ought to be out playin' footer."

"But you need twenty-two people for that," Mark pointed out, "and there's only Harriet and me. Besides, it's summer. And Harriet is a bit of a duffer at French cricker."

"Don't be impudent, boy! Gad, when I was your age I'd have been out collectin' birds' eggs."

"*Birds' eggs!*" said Mark, scandalized. "But I'm a subscribing member of the Royal Society for the Protection of Birds."

"Butterflies, then," growled his Great-Uncle.

"I read a book, Great-Uncle, that said all the butterflies were being killed by indiscriminate use of pesticides and what's left ought to be carefully preserved."

Sir Gavin was turning egg-plant colour and seemed likely to explode.

"Boy's a regular sea-lawyer," he said furiously. "Grow up into one of those confounded trade-union johnnies. Why don't you go out on your velocipede, then, sir? At your age I was as keen as mustard, by gad; used to ride miles on my penny-farthing, rain or shine."

"No bike," said Mark. "Only the unicorn, and he's got a swelled fetlock; we're fomenting it."

"Unicorn! Never heard such namby-pamby balderdash

in my life! Here," Great-Uncle Gavin said, "what's your weekly allowance when your pater's at home?"

With the disturbed family ghost and the prospect of Uncle Gavin's indefinite stay to depress them, Mr and Mrs Armitage had rather meanly decided that they were in need of three weeks in Madeira, and had left the day before.

"Half a crown a week," said Mark. "I've had three weeks in advance."

"How much does a bike cost nowadays?"

"Oh, I daresay you could pick one up for thirty-five pounds."

"*What?*" Great-Uncle Gavin nearly fell out of his chair but then, rallying, he pulled seven five-pound notes out of his ample wallet. "Here, then, boy; this is an advance on your allowance for the next two hundred and eighty weeks. I'll collect it from your governor when he comes home. Cut along, now, and buy a bicycle, an' go for a topping spin and *don't let me see your face again until supper-time.*"

"But I don't want a bicycle," Mark said.

"Be off, boy, make yourself scarce, don't argue! – On second thoughts, 'spose I'd better come with you, to make sure you don't spend the money on some appallin' book about nature."

So Great-Uncle Gavin stood over Mark while the latter unwillingly and furiously purchased a super-excellent low-slung bicycle with independent suspension, disc brakes, three-inch tyres, five-speed, and an outboard motor. None of which assets did Mark want in the least, as who would when they had a perfectly good unicorn to ride?

"Now, be off with you and see how quickly you can get to Brighton and back."

Day after day thereafter, no sooner had breakfast been eaten than Mark was hounded from the house by his relentless Great-Uncle and urged to try and better his yesterday's time to Brighton.

"Gosh, he must have led those Mbutam-Mbutas a life," he muttered darkly in the privacy of Harriet's room.

"I suppose he's old and we ought to be patient with him," Harriet said. She was pounding herbs in a mortar for her domestic science homework.

The trouble was, concluded Mark, gloomily pedalling along one afternoon through a heavy summer downpour, that during his forty years among the Mbutam-Mbutas Great-Uncle Gavin had acquired the habit of command; it was almost impossible not to obey his orders.

Almost impossible; not quite. Presently the rain increased to a cloudburst.

"Drat Great-Uncle Gavin! I'm not going all the way to Brighton in this," Mark decided. "Anyway, why *should* I go to Brighton?"

And he climbed a stile and dashed up a short grassy path to a small nearby church which had a convenient and dry-looking porch. He left his bike on the other side of the stile, for that is another disadvantage of bikes; you can never take them all the way to where you want to go.

The church proved to be chilly and not very interesting, so Mark, who always carried a paperback in his pocket, settled on the porch bench to read until the rain abated. After a while, hearing footsteps, he looked up and saw that a smallish, darkish, foreign-looking man had joined him.

"Nasty afternoon," Mark said civilly.

"Eh? Yes! Yes indeed." The man seemed nervous; he kept glancing over his shoulder down the path.

"Is your bicycle, boy, by wall yonder?" he asked by and by.

"Yes it is."

"Is a fine one," the man said. "Very fine one. Would go lickety-spit fast, I daresay?"

"An average of twenty m.p.h.," Mark said gloomily.

"Will it? Will it so?"

The little man fell silent, glancing out uneasily once more at the rainy dusk, while Mark strained his eyes to see the print of his book. He noticed that his companion seemed to be shuffling about, taking a pack off his back and rummaging among the contents; presently Mark realized that something was being held out to him. He looked up from the page and saw a golden apple – quite a large one, about the size of a Bramley. On one side the gold had a reddish bloom, as if the sun had ripened it. The other side was paler. Somebody had taken two bites out of the red side; Mark wondered what it had done to their teeth. Near the stalk was a dark-brown stain, like a patch of rust.

"Nice, eh?" the little man said, giving the apple to Mark, who nearly dropped it on the flagged floor. It must have weighed at least four pounds.

"Is it real gold all through?" he asked. "Must be quite valuable."

"Valuable?" the little man said impressively. "Such apple is beyond price. You of course well-educated, familiar with Old Testament tale of Adam and Eve?"

"W-why yes," Mark said, stammering a little. "But you – you don't mean to say *that* apple…?"

"Self-same one," the little man said, nodding his head. "Original bite marks of Adam and Eve before apple carried out of Eden. Then – see stain? Blood of Abel. Cain killed him for apple. Stain will never wash off."

"Goodness," Mark said.

"Not all, however – not all at all! Apple of discord – golden apple same which began Trojan War – have heard of such?"

"Why, yes. But – but you're not telling me—"

"Identical apple," the little man said proudly. "Apples of Asgard, too? Heard of? Scandinavian golden apples of perpetual youth, guarded by Idhuun?"

"Yes, but you don't—"

"Such was one of those. Not to mention Apples of Hesperides, stolen by Hercules."

"Hold on – surely it couldn't have been both?"

"Could," the little man said. "Was. William Tell's apple – familiar story? – same apple. Newton – apple fell on head, letting in dangerous principle of gravity. This. Atalanta – apple thrown by Milanion to stop her winning race. Also. Prince Ahmed's apple—"

"Stop, stop!" said Mark. "I don't understand how it could possibly be *all* those."

But somehow, as he held the heavy, shining thing in his hand, he did believe the little man's story. There was a peculiar, rather nasty fascination about the apple. It scared him, and yet he wanted it.

"So, see," the little man said, nodding more than ever, "worth millions pounds. No lie – millions. And yet I give to you—"

"Now, wait a minute—"

"Give in exchange for bicycle, yes? Okay?"

"Well, but – but *why*? Why don't you want the apple?"

"Want bicycle more." He glanced down the road again, and now Mark guessed.

"Someone's after you – the police? You stole the apple?"

"Not stole, no, no, no! Did swap, like with bicycle, you agree, yes?"

He was already halfway down the path. Hypnotized, Mark watched him climb the stile and mount the bike, wobbling. Suddenly Mark found his voice and called:

"What did you swap for it?"

"Drink of water – in desert, see?"

"Who's chasing you, then?"

By now the little man was chugging down the road and his last word, indistinct, floated back through the rain, something ending in '-ese'; it might have been Greek for all Mark could make of it.

He put the apple in his pocket, which sagged under the weight, and, since the shower was slackening, walked to the road to flag a lift home in the next lorry.

Great-Uncle Gavin nearly burst a blood-vessel when he learned that Mark had exchanged his new bicycle for an apple, albeit a gold one.

"Did what – merciful Providence – an *apple*? – Hesperides? Eden? Asgard? Never heard such a pack of moonshine in all me born – let's see it then. Where is it?"

Mark produced the apple and a curious gleam lit up Uncle Gavin's eye.

"Mind," he said, "don't believe a word of the feller's tale, but plain that's val'ble; far too val'ble an article to be in *your* hands, boy. Better give it here at once. I'll get Christie's to value it. And of course we must advertise in *The Times* for the wallah who palmed it off on you – highly illegal transaction, I daresay."

Mark felt curiously relieved to be rid of the apple, as if a load had been lifted from his mind as well as his pocket.

He ran upstairs whistling. Harriet, as usual, was up in her room mixing things in retorts and crucibles. When Uncle Gavin, as in duty bound, asked each evening what she had been learning that day in her domestic science course, she always replied briefly, "Spelling." "Spellin', gel? Rum notion of housekeepin' the johnny seems to have. Still, daresay it keeps you out of mischief." In fact, as Harriet had confided to Mark, Professor Grimalkin was a retired alchemist who, having failed to find the Philosopher's Stone, was obliged to take in pupils to make ends meet. He was not a very good teacher; his heart wasn't in it. Mark watched Harriet toss a pinch of green powder into a boiling beaker. Half a peach tree shot up, wavered, sagged, and then collapsed. Impatiently Harriet tipped the frothing liquid out of the window and put some more water on to boil.

Then she returned to the window and peered into the dark.

"Funny," she said. "There seem to be some people waiting outside the front door. Can't think why they didn't ring the bell. Could you let them in, Mark? My hands are all covered with prussic acid. I expect they're friends of Uncle Gavin's."

Mark went down and opened the door. Outside, dimly illuminated by the light from the porch, he saw three ladies. They seemed to be dressed in old-fashioned clothes, drainpipe skirts down to their ankles, and cloaks and bonnets rather like those of Salvation Army lasses; their bonnets were perched on thick, lank masses of hair. Mark didn't somehow care for their faces, which resembled those of dogs – but not tame domestic dogs, so much as starved, wild, slightly mad dogs; they stared at Mark hungrily.

"Er – I'm so sorry. Did you ring? Have you been waiting long?" he said.

"A long, long time. Since the world-tree was but a seed in darkness. We are the daughters of Night," one of them hollowly replied. She moved forward with a leathery rustle.

"Oh." Mark noticed that she had bats' wings. He stepped back a little. "Do you want to see Great-Uncle – Sir Gavin Armitage? Won't you come in?"

"Nay. We are the watchers by the threshold. Our place is here."

"Oh, all right. What name shall I say?"

To this question they replied in a sort of gloomy chant, taking it in turns to speak.

"We are the avengers of blood."

"Sisters of the nymph with the apple-bough, Nemesis."

"We punish the sin of child against parent –"

"Youth against age –"

"Brother against brother –"

"We are the Erinyes, the Kindly Ones –" (But their expressions were far from kindly, Mark thought.)

"Tisiphone –"

"Alecto –"

"And Megaera."

"And what did you wish to see Sir Gavin about?" Mark knew his great-uncle hated to be disturbed once he was settled in the evening with a glass of port and *The Times*.

"We attend him who holds the apple."

"There is blood on it – a brother's blood, shed by a brother."

"It cries for vengeance."

"Oh, I *see*!" said Mark, beginning to take in the situation. Now he understood why the little man had been so anxious for a bicycle. "But, look here, dash it all, Uncle Gavin hasn't shed any blood! That was Cain, and it was a long time ago. I don't see why Uncle should be responsible."

"He holds the apple."

"He must bear the guilt."

"The sins of the father are visited on the children."

"Blood calls for blood."

Then the three wolfish ladies disconcertingly burst into a sort of hymn, shaking tambourines and beating on them with brass-studded rods which they pulled out from among their draperies:

> *"We are the daughters*
> *Of darkness and time*
> *We follow the guilty*
> *We punish the crime*
> *Nothing but bloodshed*
> *Will settle old scores*
> *So blood has to flow and*
> *That blood must be yours!"*

When they had finished they fixed their ravenous eyes on Mark again and the one called Alecto said:

"Where is he?"

Mark felt greatly relieved that Uncle Gavin had taken the apple away from him and was therefore apparently

143

responsible for its load of guilt, but as this was a mean thought he tried to stifle it. Turning (not that he liked having the ladies behind his back) he went into the sitting-room where Uncle Gavin was sitting snug by the fire and said:

"There are some callers asking for you, Great-Uncle."

"God bless my soul, at this time of the evenin'? Who the deuce..."

Great-Uncle Gavin crossly stumped out to the porch, saying over his shoulder, "Why didn't you ask 'em in, boy? Not very polite to leave 'em standing –"

Then he saw the ladies and his attitude changed. He said sharply:

"Didn't you see the notice on the gate, my good women? It says NO HAWKERS OR CIRCULARS. I give handsome cheques to charity each year at Christmas and make it a rule never to contribute to door-to-door collections. So be off, if you please!"

"We do not seek money," Tisiphone hungrily replied.

"Milk-bottle tops, jumble, old gold, it's all the same. Pack of meddlesome old maids – I've no time for you!" snapped Sir Gavin. "Good night!" And he shut the door smartly in their faces.

"Have to be firm with that sort of customer," he told Mark. "Become a thorough nuisance otherwise – tiresome old harpies. Got wind of that golden apple, I daresay – shows what happens when you mix with such people. Shockin' mistake. Take the apple to Christie's tomorrow.

Now, please see I'm not disturbed again." And he returned to the sitting-room.

Mark looked uneasily at the front door but it remained shut; evidently the three Kindly Ones were content to wait outside. But there they stayed; when Mark returned to Harriet's room he looked out of the window and saw them, sombre and immovable, in the shadows outside the porch, evidently prepared to sit out the night.

"Not very nice if they're going to picket our front door from now on," he remarked gloomily to Harriet. "Goodness knows what the postman will think. And *I* don't fancy 'em above half. Wonder how we can get rid of them."

"I've an idea," Harriet said. "Professor Grimalkin was talking about them the other day. They are the Furies. But it's awfully hard to shake them off once they're after you."

"That's jolly."

"There are various things you can do, biting off your finger —"

"Some hope of Uncle Gavin doing that!"

"Or shaving your head."

"Wouldn't be much use, since he's bald as a bean already."

"You can bathe seven times in running water or the blood of pigs —"

"He always *does* take a lot of cold baths and we had pork for supper, so plainly that's no go."

"Well, you can go into exile for a year," Harriet said.

"I only wish he would."

"Or build them a grotto, nice and dark, preferably under an ilex tree, and make suitable offerings."

"Such as what?"

"Anything black, or they rather go for iris flowers. Milk and honey too. And they can be shot with a bow of horn, but that doesn't seem to be very successful as a rule."

"Oh well, let's try the milk and honey and something black for now," Mark said. "And I'll make a bow of horn tomorrow – I've got Candleberry's last year's horn in my room somewhere." Candleberry was the unicorn.

Harriet therefore collected a black velvet pincushion and a bowl of milk and honey. These she put out on the front step, politely wishing the Daughters of Night good evening, to which their only response was a baleful silence.

Next morning the milk and honey was still there. So were the Furies. Evidently they did not intend to be placated so easily. By daylight they were even less prepossessing, having black claws, bloodshot eyes, and snakes for hair. However, slipping down early to remove he saucer in case the postman tripped over it, Harriet did notice that all the pins had been removed from the pincushion. And eaten? This was encouraging. So was the fact that when the postman arrived with a card from their parents in Madeira – 'Having wonderful time hope you are behaving yourselves' – he walked clean through the Furies without noticing them at all. Evidently his conscience at least was clear.

"Perhaps they're only visible to relatives of their

victims," Harriet suggested to Mark, who was working on the unicorn horn with emery paper.

"I hope they've taken the pins to stick in Uncle Gavin," he growled. In default of bicycle exercise Great-Uncle Gavin had made Mark do five hundred press-ups before breakfast and had personally supervised the operation. Mark felt it would be far, far better to shoot Uncle Gavin than the Furies who, after all, were only doing their duty.

The most annoying thing of all was that, after his initial interview with them, Uncle Gavin seemed not to notice the avenging spirits at all ("He only sees what he chooses to," Harriet guessed) and walked past them quite as unconcernedly as the postman had. He packed up the golden apple in a cigar-box, rang for a taxi, and departed to London. The Furies followed him in a black, muttering group, and were seen no more for several hours; Mark and Harriet heaved sighs of relief. Prematurely, though; at tea-time the Furies reappeared, even blacker, muttering still more, and took up their post once more by the front door.

"Lost the old boy somewhere in London," Mark diagnosed. "Or perhaps they were chucked out of Christie's."

The unwanted guests were certainly in a bad mood. This time they were accompanied by a smallish thick-set winged serpent or dragon who seemed to be called Ladon. Harriet heard them saying, "Down, Ladon! Behave yourself, and soon you shall sup on blood." Ladon too seemed to have a snappish disposition, and nearly took off Harriet's hand when she stooped to pat him on returning home from her domestic science lesson.

"What a beautiful green his wings are. Is he yours?" she said to the Furies politely.

"He is the guardian of the apple; he but waits for his own," Tisiphone replied dourly.

Ladon did not share the Furies' scruples about coming indoors; evidently he was used to a warmer clime and found the doorstep too draughty. He followed Harriet into the kitchen and flopped his bulky length in front of the stove, hissing cantankerously at anyone who came near, and thoroughly upsetting Walrus, the cat.

Walrus was not the only one.

"Miss Harriet! Get that nasty beast out of here at once!" exclaimed Mrs Epis, the cook, when she came back from shopping. "And what those black ladies are doing out on the front doorstep, I'm sure *I* don't know; I've two or three times give them a hint to be off but they won't take it."

Evidently Mrs Epis counted as one of the family or else she, too, had a guilty conscience. Mark and Harriet soon found that visitors to the house who had episodes in their past of which they had cause to be ashamed were apt to notice the Erinyes in a patchy, nervous way and hurry away with uneasy glances behind them, or else break into sudden and embarrassing confessions.

And Ladon was a thorough nuisance. So long as Harriet kept on the fan heater in her room he would lie in front of it, rolling luxuriously on his back and only snapping if anyone approached him. But at bed-time when she turned the fan off – for she hated a warm room at night – he became fretful and roamed snarling and clanking about the house. Even Uncle Gavin tripped over him then and blamed the children furiously for leaving what he thought was a rolled-up tent lying in the passage.

"Things can't go on like this," Mark said despondently.

"We've certainly got to get rid of them all somehow before Mother and Father come home next week," Harriet agreed. "And Uncle Gavin's plainly going to be no help at all."

Uncle Gavin was even more tetchy than usual. Christie's had sent him a letter saying that in view of the apple's unique historical interest it was virtually impossible to put a price on it, but in their opinion it was certainly worth well over a million pounds. They would return the apple by the next registered post, pending further instructions. And the advertisement which appeared in *The Times* every day – 'Will person who persuaded young boy to exchange valuable new bicycle for metal apple on August 20 please contact Box XXX' – was producing no replies.

"Nor likely to," Mark said. "That chap knows when he's well out of trouble."

During that day Mark finished his horn bow and tried shooting at the Furies with it. The operation was a total failure. The arrows, which he had after all made out of a fallow-deer's antler (brow, bay and tray), were curved and flew on a bias, like bowls, missing the visitors nine times out of ten. If they did hit they merely passed clean through and, as Mark told Harriet later, he felt a fool having to pick them up under the malign snakey-and-bonneted gaze of Alecto, Megaera and Tisiphone.

Harriet, however, came home in good spirits. She pulled out and showed Mark a paper covered with Professor Grimalkin's atrocious handwriting.

"What is it?" he asked.

"Recipe for a friendship philtre. You've heard of a love philtre? This is like that, only milder. I'm going to try it in their milk. Now don't interrupt, while I make it up."

She put her crucible on to bubble. Mark curled up at the end of her bed and read his bird book, only coming out when Harriet tripped over Ladon and dratted him, or asked Mark's opinion about the professor's handwriting.

"Is this 'verdigris' or 'verjuice', do you think? And is that 'Add sugar', or 'Allow to simmer'?"

"It'll be a miracle if the stuff turns out all right," Mark said pessimistically. "Anyway, do we *want* the Furies friendly?"

"Of course we do, it'll be a tremendous help. Where was I now? Add bad egg, and brown under grill."

Finally the potion was finished and put in a cough-mixture bottle. ("It smells awful," Mark said, sniffing. "Never mind, how do we know what *they* like?") A spoonful of the noxious stuff was divided between three bowls of milk, which were placed on the front step, at the feet of the unresponsive Erinyes.

However after a moment or two they began to snuff the air like bloodhounds on the track of a malefactor, and as Harriet tactfully retired she had the pleasure of seeing all three of them lapping hungrily at the mixture. So far, at least, the spell had worked. Harriet went hopefully to bed.

Next morning she was woken by a handful of earth flung at her window.

"Miss Harriet!" It was Mrs Epis on the lawn. "Miss Harriet, you'll have to make the breakfast yourself. I'm taking a week's holiday. And things had better be different when I come back or I'll give in my notice; you can tell your Ma it was me broke the Crown Derby teapot and I'm sorry about it, but there's some things a body can't bear. Now I'm off home."

Sleepy and mystified, Harriet went to the kitchen to put on the kettle for Great-Uncle Gavin's tea. There, to her dismay, she found the Furies, who greeted her with toothy smiles. They were at ease in basket-chairs round the stove, with their long skirts turned back so as to toast their skinny legs and feet, which rested on Ladon. Roused by the indoor warmth, the snakes on their heads were in a state of disagreeable squirm and writhe, which Harriet too found hard to bear, particularly before breakfast; she quite sympathized with the cook's departure.

"Oh, good morning," she said, however, stoutly controlling her qualms. "Would you like some more milk?" She mixed another brew with potion (which was graciously accepted) and took up a tray of breakfast to Great-Uncle

Gavin, explaining that Mrs Epis had been called away. By the time she returned, Mark was in the kitchen glumly taking stock of the situation.

"Feel like a boiled egg?" Harriet said.

"I'll do it, thanks. I've had enough of your domestic science."

They ate their boiled eggs in the garden. But they had taken only a bite or two when they were startled by hysterical screams from the window-cleaner who, having arrived early and started work on the kitchen window, had looked through the glass and was now on his knees in the flower-bed, confessing to anyone who would listen that he had pinched a diamond brooch from an upstairs bedroom in West Croydon. Before he was pacified they had also to deal with the man who came to mend the fridge, who seemed frightfully upset about something he had done to a person called Elsie, as well as a French onion-seller who dropped eight strings of onions in the back doorway and fled, crying, "*Mon dieu, mon Dieu, mon crime est decouvert! Je suis perdu!*"

"This won't do," said Mark, as he returned from escorting the sobbing electrician to the gate. Exhaustedly mopping his brow he didn't look where he was going, barked his shins painfully on Ladon, who was stalking the cat, and let out an oath. It went unheard; the Furies, much cheered by their breakfast and a night spent in the snug kitchen, were singing their bloodthirsty hymn fortissimo, with much clashing of tambourines. Ladon and the cat seemed all set for a duel to the death; and Great-Uncle Gavin was bawling down the stairs for less row while a man was breakfastin', dammit!

"It's all right," Harriet soothed Mark. "I knew the potion would work wonders. Now, your Kindlinesses," she said to the Erinyes, "we've got a beautiful grotto ready for you, just the sort of place you like, except I'm sorry there isn't an ilex tree, if you wouldn't mind stepping this way," and she led them to the coal-cellar, which, being peaceful and dark, met with their entire approval.

"I daresay they'll be glad of a nap," she remarked, shutting the door thankfully on them. "After all, they've been unusually busy lately."

"That's all very well," said Mark. "They better not stay there long. *I'm* the one that fetches the coal. And there's still beastly Ladon to dispose of."

Ladon, unlike his mistresses, was not tempted by milk containing a friendship potion. His nature remained as intractable as ever. He now had the cat Walrus treed on the banister post at the top of the stairs, and was coiled in a baleful bronze-and-gold heap just below, hissing like a pressure-cooker.

"Perhaps bone arrows will work on *him*," said Mark, and dashed to his bedroom.

As he reappeared a lot of things happened at once.

The postman rang the front-door bell and handed Harriet a letter for Uncle Gavin and a registered parcel labelled GOLD WITH CARE. Ladon made a dart at the cat, who countered with a faster-than-light left hook, all claws extended. It caught the dragon in his gills and he let out a screech like the whistle of a steam locomotive, which fetched the Furies from their grotto at the double, brass-studded batons out and snakes ready to strike.

At the same moment Mark let fly with his bow and arrow and Uncle Gavin burst from his bedroom exclaiming, "I *will* not have this bedlam while I'm digestin' my breakfast!" He received the arrow intended for Ladon full in his slippered heel and gave a yell which quite drowned the noise made by the cat and the dragon.

"Who did that? Who fired that damned thing?" Enraged, hopping, Uncle Gavin pulled out the bone dart. "What's that cat doin' up there? Why's this confounded reptile in the house? Who are those people down there? *What the devil's going on around here?*"

Harriet gave a shout of joy.

"Look, quick!" she called to the Furies. "Look at his heel! It's bleeding!" (It was indeed.) "You said blood had to flow and now it has, so you've done your job and can leave with clear consciences! Quick, Mark, open the parcel and give that wretched dragon his apple and they can *all* leave. Poor Uncle Gavin, is your foot very painful? Mark didn't mean to hit you. I'll bandage it up in two shakes."

Mark tore the parcel undone and tossed the golden apple to Ladon, who caught it with a snap of his jaws and was gone in a flash through the landing window. (It was shut, but no matter.) At the same moment the Furies, their lust for vengeance appeased by the sight of Uncle Gavin's gore, departed with more dignity by the front door.

Alecto even turned and gave Harriet a ghastly smile.

"Thank you for having us, child," she said. "We enjoyed our visit."

"Don't mention it," Harriet mechanically replied, and only just stopped herself from adding, "Come again."

Then she sat her great-uncle in the kitchen armchair and bathed his heel. The wound, luckily, proved to be no more than a scratch. While she bandaged it he read his letter, and suddenly gave a curious grunt, of pleasure and astonishment.

"God bless my soul! They want me back! Would you believe it!"

"Who want you back, Great-Uncle?" Harriet asked, tying the ends of the bandage in a knot.

"The Mbutam-Mbutas, bless 'em! They want me to go and help 'em as Military and Economic Adviser. I've always said there's good in the black feller and I say so yet! Well, well, well! Don't know when I've been so pleased." He gave his nose a tremendous blow and wiped his eyes.

"Oh, Uncle Gavin, how perfectly splendid!" Harriet gave him a hug. "When do they want you to go?"

"Three weeks' time. Bless my soul, I'll have a bustle getting me kit ready."

"Oh, we'll all help like mad. I'll run down the road now and fetch Mrs Epis; I'm sure she'll be glad to come back for such an emergency."

Mrs Epis had no objection at all, once she was assured the intruders were gone from the house.

Harriet had one startled moment when they got back to the house.

"Uncle Gavin!" she called, and ran upstairs. The old gentleman had out his tin tropical trunk and was inspecting a pith helmet. "Yes, m'dear, what is it?" he said absently.

"The little brown bottle on the kitchen table. Was it – did you – you...?"

"Oh, that? My cough mixture? Yes, I finished it and threw the bottle away. Why, though, bless my soul – *there's* my cough mixture! What the deuce have I been an' taken, then, gel? Anything harmful?"

"Oh no, perfectly harmless," Harriet hastily reassured him. "Now, you give me anything you want mended and I'll be getting on with it."

" 'Pon my soul," Uncle Gavin said, pulling out a bundle of spotless white ducks and a dress-jacket with tremendous epaulettes and fringes, " 'pon my soul, I believe I'll miss you young ones when I'm back in the tropics. Come and visit me sometimes, m'dear? Young Mark too. Where is the young rogue? Ho, ho, can't help laughing when I think how he hit me in the heel. Who'd have thought he had it in him?"

"He's gone apple-picking at the farm down the road," Harriet explained. "He wants to earn enough to pay back that thirty-five pounds."

"Good lad, good lad!" Uncle Gavin exclaimed approvingly. "Not that he need have bothered, mark you."

And in fact, when Mark tried to press the money on Uncle Gavin at his departure, he would have none of it.

"No, no, bless your little hearts, split it between you." He chucked Harriet under the chin and earnestly shook Mark's hand. "I'd never have thought I'd cotton to young 'uns as I have to you two – 'mazing thing. So you keep the money and buy something pretty to remind you of my visit."

But Mark and Harriet thought they would remember his visit quite easily without that – especially as the Furies had taken quite a fancy to the coal-cellar and frequently came back to occupy it on chilly winter nights.

Nine

THE LILAC IN THE LAKE

THERE WAS THIS old boy, Enoch Dibben, the schoolmaster at a little place at the back of beyond. Grydale, it's called, likely you'll not have heard of it. The lads at that village are terrible teasers, to a boy; sure as one of them looks you in the eye, it's because he's dropped a live eel in your lunch-basket, or loosed a sackful of grasshoppers inside your car, or tied your shoe-laces together so that you fall over when you try to walk. Teasers, and artful, they are, but not an ounce of vice in them. Indeed, Mr Dibben rather enjoyed their goings-on. He was such a dreamy old fellow, wandering about the dale with his hands behind his back and his head in the clouds, that it was someway pleasant for him to feel folk noticed he was there to the extent of filling his inkwell with golden syrup, as Charlie Herdman did one Friday afternoon. For he was a single man, and sometimes felt a bit lonely, with no one to warm his slippers or fry his bacon, or bake him a bit of parkin for a Sunday treat.

It's a quiet little place, Grydale, thirty miles from the nearest railway. Up above it on each side the fells climb out of sight. After the sun goes down you can hear a pheasant cluck in Grassy Woods, five miles off, or a dog barking in Shipton, down at the foot of the valley.

Sometimes at night in his little stone cottage Mr Dibben, snug in bed, would think he heard a tapping at the door. Specially of a milky summer night, when you could hardly tell if the noise that broke the silence was the stream whispering or your own heart beating, he used to think somebody quietly knocked at his door: he used to think he could hear voices calling, "Mr Dibben! Mr Dibben! Please come down and let us in! We're so lonely and cold! Let us in, and we'll cook for you and clean for you, we'll dig your garden and darn your socks, we'll wash your shirts and tidy your papers and bake your bread and sharpen your pencils!"

Mr Dibben, though, took no notice of this, except maybe to burrow deeper in the bedclothes. It's those naughty boys, he would think, shutting his eyes tight; they want me to come down and open the door; then a bucket of potato peelings will probably fall on my head while they run off up to the village laughing themselves into hiccups; I'm not such a fool as *that*!

Sometimes of a morning when he opened his eyes and the blue day came rushing in he'd wonder if he had dreamed the voices; sometimes he'd resolve that next time he heard them he'd go down to the door and open it. But somehow he never did.

There were only three cars in Grydale; Mr Dibben's old Rattler was one of them. The boys left his car alone, whatever else they did, they never played any of their tricks on Rattler; when you live so cut-off you get to treat cars with respect. So, on fine week-ends and summer evenings, Mr Dibben was a great wanderer, you might come across him anywhere about the countryside from Mickle Fell to Spurn Head. What was he doing? Hunting for legends. If he heard tell of a village where they'd a bewitched bakehouse, or where the hares danced in a ring on Midsummer Eve, or where the ghost of King Richard sat eating gooseberries in the churchyard, first free moment Mr Dibben had he'd be off, fast as old Rattler could make it at a galloping eighteen miles an hour. And once there he'd get the whole tale out of the oldest inhabitants – or the youngest – or whoever had a fancy to sit in the sun spinning tall tales. Mr Dibben wrote them all down on sheets of paper with holes at one side and stuck them in a book. Bigger than the Bible it would be, when finished, and he was that proud of it! "When it's published," he used to say, "my name will be known throughout the length and breadth of England." But there were some in the village used to think he'd better get a move on, sending it to a publisher, or one of these days he'd find himself knocking at St Peter's gate with all his bits of paper still under his arm. And no one's yet said if they publish books in heaven. Though most likely they do, or what should we all do for a read on a sunny afternoon in the fields of Eden?

There's many stories in our countryside; one grows out of another as quick as groundsel. If a farmer has a dog that's trained to answer the phone, or someone's house falls down because the builder forgot the mortar, or a boggart sits with the family in the evenings, playing Scrabble and forecasting the winner of the Derby, you may be sure the news will get all over the village in a twinkling, and from there, embroidered up a bit, to the four corners of the county, even as far away as Nottingham.

So Mr Dibben was well occupied, chasing far and wide like a pup after bumble-bees, and it wasn't till he'd been in Grydale nigh on ten year that he found, with all his questings and questionings, he'd clean missed one of the best tales of all, and that on his own doorstep, the tale of the Grydale Singers.

Charlie Herdman told it to him then, one hot sleepy afternoon after school. Charlie had a reason for this: he wanted to keep Mr Dibben distracted and out of the way up in the schoolhouse while some friends of his prepared a little surprise. So he said to the old boy, as they were tidying up the Infants' books – Charlie was monitor that week –

"I wonder you aren't afeared to live in that house of yourn, all on your own down below the village, Mester Dibben. Don't you never think the Grydale Singers might spirit you away?"

"Grydale Singers?" says Mr Dibben, all agog at once.

"What are they? Grydale Singers, I don't believe I've ever heard of them. Leave rubbing the blackboard, my boy – I'll do that – now you tell me about these Grydale Singers."

And he commences rubbing at the board with his handkerchief.

"Well," artful Charlie says, thoroughly enjoying himself now, "it's a tale we have in the village about these seven sisters who lived here in my grandfather's time, or it may have been in *his* granfer's time, I ain't so special sure, but it was in the days when folk rode horseback and the summers was always hot and mushrooms grew on the village green and lasses wore their hair hanging long and loose down their backs."

"Seven sisters – yes, yes," Mr Dibben he says. "Just a minute, Charlie, while I give the tape-recorder a bit of a bang – it's stuck again."

For Mr Dibben had this tape-recorder he used for taking down the stories he collected, and also for teaching the children in school and trying to make them say their a's long and droopy, like an old bell-wether, instead of short and crisp like a snapped stick. He'd bought it second-hand in Leeds and tinkered about with it till it worked well enough, but times it was a bit temperamental and when he played it back instead of the voice you expected it would give you a bit of the Shipton Orpheus Choir's rendering of 'For unto us a child is born' or the frogs croaking in Malham Tarn.

"Right, Charlie, I've got it going again – now tell me about those seven sisters. What were their names?"

"Why," Charlie says, "there's some believe it wasn't seven sisters but three, or maybe four, but the way I heard it there's seven of 'em, and their names was Mary, Mercy, Marila, Martha, Marian, Marjorie, and Marigold, and they was the blacksmith's lasses, Mr Artingstall it was then, and pretty as a podful of young peas. Fair hair, blue eyes, and all that. Half the lads in the village was after them. They lived in the blacksmith's cottage, that's the one you have now, Mr Dibben, afore my granda's grandad bought it up, and they used to help their dad with blowing the bellows and suchlike. Pretty as they were, they was that uppish and standoffish they'd sworn none of them 'ud ever marry, not a one of them could abide the male sex. Spinsters to their deathbeds they declared they'd be, on account of all the teasing they'd gone through at school, the lads in Grydale – as you know – being fond of a lark."

"Seven sisters sworn not to marry – yes, yes," Mr Dibben says, setting light to the blackboard rubber instead of his pipe. "This is most interesting, Charlie, go on. What happened to them?"

"They used to sing a lot – any party or wedding, funeral or christening there was in the village the Artingstall lasses would be on hand obliging with a bit of Stainer or whatever was suitable. And of an evening they'd sit under the lilac bush in the garden – the same one that's still there now, Mr Dibben – singing away like a sipkin of thrushes. Well, about the time Mary, that's the eldest one, was getting on for twenty-three and folk had started to think maybe they'd stick to their word and really would end up as old maids, people began to notice that when they sang a chorus, one of 'em was always flat. And next thing they found was that Mary had been secretly running off to meet a young fellow, name of Huxtable, kind of a wandering pedlar who came up to the village once a month with ribbons and saucepans, and next thing was, he and Mary had got wed. Well, the other sisters put a good face on it, they sang at her wedding, but they felt she'd let the family down, they swore *they'd* never do such a thing. In fact it made them more set against men than ever, they reckoned Huxtable had fair bewitched her. I forget whether he took her to Scunthorpe or Skegness or Scarborough for the honeymoon but anyhow, not long after they got back they went out one day fishing on Grydale Water, in a rowboat, and Mary somehow got her long hair caught in the anchor chain, was pulled overboard with it, down to the bottom, and drowned. Her husband was fair mazed with grief, some say he jumped right overboard after her and that was the end of him, others that he joined the French Foreign Legion and was seen in Whitby twenty years after, declaring that he was the Emperor Boneypart. Anyway he never came back to Grydale."

"What became of the other sisters?"

"The very night after she was drowned they went out to the lilac tree for the last time and sang a lament for her, folk who heard it said it was so sad that the owls in the churchyard were boo-hooing too, and the lilac tree dropped all its blossom for pity. And when they'd done, they all got up and walked into Grydale Water and that was the end of *them*."

"Really?" says Mr Dibben, absent-mindedly putting his ballpoint in his mouth and his lighted pipe in his pocket. "Dear me, what a remarkable tale. Is that the end of it, Charlie?"

"Not quite," Charlie says. "For there's folk as says that from that day to this, every night from half-past eleven to twelve midnight, those sisters can be heard under the lilac tree singing their lament – only they won't do it if there's a man within earshot because they're still fell set against the whole flaysome race. It's said they'll go on lamenting till trout swim in Grassy Wood, or till a man can be found that'll walk into Grydale Water for love of them."

"Dear me," Mr Dibben said again. "So they won't sing when a man's about? Are there ladies in the village that have heard them, then?"

"My mam says she has, many a time," Charlie says. "When she's been coming home late from the Ladies' Glee Club or the Bingo Drive."

"I must go and see your good mother without delay," says Mr Dibben, trying to lock up his desk with a bit of blackboard chalk.

Before he left he gave Charlie a present – a pencil-case it was, made of red-painted tin and shaped like a rocket. When you twisted the bottom round, strips of numbers up the side worked out the multiplication table for you, all the way from one times one to nine times nine. "That's for you,

Charlie, my boy, as a reward for such an exceedingly interesting piece of lore."

"No, no, Mr Dibben, I don't want anything, honest I don't."

Charlie was a bit upset at being given a present, and such a handsome one too. But Mr Dibben insisted, and then he hurried off to ask all the womenfolk in the village if they'd ever heard the Grydale Singers. Some said yes, some said no, some said they didn't believe in such foolishness. Time Mr Dibben went home it was getting towards dusk, the swifts had stopped scooping for flies and gone to roost in the eaves.

He opened his gate, gave a bit of a glance at the historic lilac bush, never noticed the hedge, which heaved and shook with giggles because half the boys of the village were lodged in it, and went on to open his front door, which led straight into the little parlour. He found the door uncommon hard to shift, and when at last he got it open, about a ton of water surged out at him. The boys had been busy ever since school finished, filling his room full of river through a hosepipe led from Grydale Falls. Mr Dibben's cottage, the only house below the falls, was well downhill from the village, so it was easy enough to do.

The old chap wasn't angry about it, only astonished. He stood scratching his head, while the water pushed past him down the garden path like brown coffee-suds.

"Dear have mercy!" says he to himself. "Can I have left the kitchen tap on?"

So like an old puzzled bird he looked, as he stood there on one leg, scratching his head, an old bird with its feathers all ruffled up, that the boys, who were as good-natured a set of young addlepates as you could hope to find, hadn't the heart to leave him to clear up the mess. They came bursting out of the hedge, half choked with laughing, patted Mr Dibben, picked him up, carried him into his kitchen which was still dry, and started mopping down the parlour floor.

"Eh, dear, Mr Dibben, didn't you ever guess?" Charlie said to him. "Didn't you ever wonder why I was keeping you so long at the school?"

"But then, that story you told me about the singers – was that not a true tale, Charlie?"

"The Grydale Singers? Yes, that was a canty tale enough," Charlie told him. "I daresay they'd be singing away now if we wasn't about."

Relieved to hear this, which was the only thing that had worried him, Mr Dibben went to his bed, leaving the boys to get on with swabbing down the parlour. Next day the place was still damp enough, and he thought it right to go along to Farmer Herdman, who was his landlord, and explain what had happened. Farmer Herdman shook his head over the tale (though he couldn't forbear a grin, having been a boy himself once) and offered to give them all a dusting if Mr Dibben wished. But the old boy shook his head.

"I don't hold it agen them," he says. "Young blood will out. I only thought fit to mention it, Mr Herdman, to explain how the house came to be so uncommon damp."

"As to that," Farmer Herdman he says, "the house'll be damper still soon enough. I was going to come and see you, Mester Dibben, about that very thing."

Then he began explaining something about the new dam at Shipton to the schoolmaster, who didn't hear a single word he said. For a grand notion had just come into Mr Dibben's head: why not try to get a recording of the Grydale Singers on his tape machine? Likely enough the young ladies had never heard of a tape-recorder and would have no suspicions of it, might not even notice it quietly spinning away, if he hid it under the grass and leaves. And if they did happen to spot it – well, a tape-recorder's not the same as a man, is it, no reason why that should stop them singing? As you might imagine, Mr Dibben, who used to sing himself when he was young, baritone in the Bottlewell Male Voice Choir, was mortal keen to be the first man to hear those poor sorrowful singers, and he thought he had hit on the very answer to the problem. The only snag was that he himself would have to clear out for a night and go well away so that his presence wouldn't put a cramp in the business. Where could he go? he wondered, and then he remembered his Auntie Sarah in York. She would put him up, and willing.

"So do you want to see about getting the furniture shifted, or will you leave it to me?" says Farmer Herdman, finishing his long explanation, and Mr Dibben, who hadn't taken in a word of it, quickly says, "Oh, I will, I'll look after it, thank 'ee," for he didn't want anybody meddling around the cottage while he was away and maybe upsetting the Singers. He put his hat on inside out, and bustled off home to pack up a few things.

Late that night, about twenty past eleven, he set off, first hiding the tape-recorder under the lilac tree in a clump of fern where he hoped the ghostly sisters wouldn't notice it. The tape was a two-hour one, so he calculated there would be enough and to spare for recording the lament.

Away he drove, along the side of the valley, past Grydale Water, glimmering in the hazy moonlight, and made his way to York city where, as it chanced, he found his Auntie Sarah on her deathbed, and not before it was time, either, since she was nigh on a hundred.

"Don't forget to wind the clock when I'm gone, Enoch Dibben," she croaked at him. "I've left you all my money, Enoch, on condition you have this house turned into a cat's home. Now I must be on my way – I'm ten minutes late already. My old crony Nancy Thorpe is waiting for me up there in Paradise; I promised to take her all the latest knitting patterns," and with that she took and died. Mr Dibben was a bit put out, since he was now obliged to stay in York, make arrangements for the funeral, see to moving the pusses into their new home, not to mention winding the clock. A fortnight it took him getting everything straight, and a marble slab for Auntie Sarah with half a cherub on it. He was in a fret, too, about how his tape-recorder was standing the weather, though to be sure he'd left it in a waterproof cover.

Soon as the cats were in, and a caretaker to feed them and wind the clock, he was off, hotfoot, back to Grydale, where things had not been standing still as you shall hear.

It was late night again when Mr Dibben drove back up the daleside; the mist stood in the bottom of the valley like clumps of thistledown, and the night was so quiet that old Rattler's chug-chug sounded louder than cannon-fire. Mr Dibben felt a bit lonesome thinking of the cats all snug together in their new home, and Auntie Sarah so cosy up in Paradise a-chatting with Mrs Thorpe over their plain-and-pearl, while he had only his cold empty cottage waiting for him.

When he reached the track turning down off the main road to his own house he was a bit perplexed because there seemed to be water across the road, though with all the mist lying it was hard to be sure.

"Dang it," says Mr Dibben, "are my eyes deceiving me? Surely to gracious the lake can't have risen all that much? There's not been a drop of rain in York for the last fortnight. Can it be those boys up to their tricks again?"

He stopped Rattler in the middle of the track, got out, and ambled forward on foot.

"My eyes *must* be deceiving me," he says then. "It must be some kind of a mirage. Because if the water is up here, where I think I see it, then my house is under the lake up to the chimney-pots – which is out of the question. For if my house is under water up to the chimneys, then my tape-recorder would be under water also – which is not to be thought of. I am having a hallucination," he says, "but I will ignore it."

On he goes, up to his ankles first, then up to his knees. Then he was wading with his belt under water, then his chin was covered, and at last Mr Dibben was clean gone under the water, plodding forward in search of his tape-recorder, and naught left visible but a trail of bubbles.

Well! When he got to his front gate a perfect chorus of voices greeted him.

"Evening, Mr Dibben!"

"Welcome home, then, Mr Dibben!"

"We've got your slippers a-warming, Mr Dibben!"

"And a pot of tea mashed!"

"And a rasher of bacon frying!"

"And a lovely bit of parkin in the oven!"

"And the best cheese-cakes and marmalade this side of Doncaster!"

Then they all said together, "Oh, Mr Dibben, we're *so* pleased you've come home!"

Mr Dibben was fair bewildered, as you can imagine, by such a welcome, but he couldn't help being pleased too, not a doubt of that. It was plain that the Artingstall lasses had grown tired of their solitary life and wanted someone to take care of. The only thing that worried him was, what had become of his recording of the lament, under all that lake-water, but Mercy Artingstall told him, "To tell you the truth, Mr Dibben, we was so cast down and low-spirited the night we thought you'd gone off and left us, that we never sang a note. But," she says, "we'll make up for that now!"

Of course next day in Grydale village they was fair upset to find Mr Dibben's old Rattler standing on the edge of the new reservoir, and him nowhere to be seen.

"I blame myself, that I do!" says Farmer Herdman. "I should have made certain sure that he knew about the dam they was building at valley-foot, and how the reservoir would cover his cottage. I should have moved his furniture myself into the new little house I had ready for him up in the village. I ought to have remembered what an absent-minded old chap he was. I'm right downhearted, and that's the truth."

As for Charlie Herdman, he went about the place with a face as long as an eight-day clock, and declared he'd keep the red tin pencil-case all his life in memory of poor old Mr Dibben. And Farmer Herdman said he'd have the book of tales (which they found in old Rattler) printed up in big print, with fine coloured pictures, at his own expense, as a memorial.

But they needn't have worried about keeping Mr Dibben's memory green. Punctual that night at half-past eleven, the Grydale Singers started up over the lake, over the lilac bush that was now drowned eighteen foot deep in Grydale Water – and this time they'd a baritone with them as well. And no nonsense about not singing if there was a man within earshot – the noise they made, with a rousing good rendering of the Hallelujah Chorus, was enough to fetch the whole village out of its beds, and it was the same each night after and ever since.

In fact, though there's no denying it draws the tourist business, coaches come from as far afield as Hull, some of the folk in Grydale are beginning to grumble about the nightly choruses, and have even written to the County Council to complain.

But the Council say that nothing can be done.

Ten

HARRIET'S HAIRLOOM

"OH, MOTHER," HARRIET said as she did every year. "Can't I open my birthday presents at breakfast?"

And as she did every year, Mrs Armitage replied,

"Certainly not! You know perfectly well that you weren't born till half-past four. You get your birthday presents at tea-time, not before."

"We could change the custom now we're in our teens," Harriet suggested cunningly. "You know you hate having to get up at half-past two in the morning for Mark's presents."

But Mark objected strongly to any change, and Mrs Armitage added:

"In any case, don't forget that as it's your thirteenth birthday you have to be shown into the Closed Room; there'd never be time to do that before school. Go and collect your schoolbooks now, and, Mark, wash the soot from behind your ears; if you must hunt for Lady Anne's pearls in the chimney, I wish you'd clean up before coming to breakfast."

"You'd be as pleased as anyone else if I found them," Mark grumbled, going off to put sooty marks all over the towels.

"What do you suppose is in the Closed Room?" Mark said later, as he and Harriet walked to the school bus. "I think it's a rotten swindle that only girls in the family are allowed to go inside when they get to be thirteen. Suppose it's a monster like at Glamis, what'll you do?"

"Tame it," said Harriet promptly. "I shall feed it on bread and milk and lettuce."

"That's hedgehogs, dope! Suppose it has huge teeth and tentacles and a poisonous sting three yards long?"

"Shut up! Anyway I don't suppose it is a monster. After all we never see Mother going into the Closed Room with bowls of food. It's probably just some mouldering old great-aunt in her coffin or something boring like that."

Still, it was nice to have a Closed Room in the family, Harriet reflected, and she sat in the bus happily speculating about what it might contain — jewels, perhaps, rubies as big as tomatoes, or King Arthur's sword Excalibur, left with the Armitage family for safe keeping when he went off to Avalon, or the Welsh bard Taliesin, fallen asleep in the middle of a poem — or a Cockatrice — or the vanished crew of the *Marie Céleste*, playing cards and singing shanties —

Harriet was still in a dreamy state when school began.

The first lesson was geography with old Mr Gubbins so there was no need to pay attention; she sat trying to think of suitable pet names for Cockatrices until she heard a stifled sobbing on her left.

"... is of course the Cathay of the ancients," Mr Gubbins was rambling on. "Marco Polo in his travels..."

Harriet looked cautiously round and saw that her best friend and left-hand neighbour Desirée, or Dizzry as everyone called her, was crying bitterly, hunched over the inkwell on her desk so that the tears ran into it.

Dizzry was the daughter of Ernie Perrow, the village chimney-sweep; the peculiarity of the Perrow family was that none of them ever grew to be more than six inches high. Dizzry travelled to school every day in Harriet's pocket and instead of sitting at her desk in the usual way had a small table and chair, which Mark had obligingly made her out of matchboxes, on the top of it.

"What's the matter?" whispered Harriet. "Here, don't cry into the ink – you'll make it weaker than it is already. Haven't you a handkerchief?"

She pulled sewing things out of her own desk, snipped a shred off the corner of a tablecloth she was embroidering, and passed it to Dizzry, who gulped, nodded, took a deep breath, and wiped her eyes on it.

"What's the matter?" Harriet asked again.

"It was what Mr Gubbins said that started me off," Dizzry muttered. "Talking about Cathay. Our Min always used to say she'd a fancy to go to Cathay. She'd got it muddled up with *café*. She thought she'd get cake and raspberryade and ice-cream there."

"Well, so what?" said Harriet, who saw nothing to cry about in that.

"Haven't you heard? We've lost her – we've lost our Min!"

"Oh, my goodness! You mean she's dead?"

"No, not *died*. Just lost. Nobody's seen her since yesterday breakfast time!"

Harriet privately thought this ought to have been rather a relief for the family but was too polite to say so. Min, the youngest of the Perrow children, was a perfect little fiend, always in trouble of one kind or another. When not engaged in entering sweet jars in the village shop and stealing Butter Kernels or Quince Drops, she was probably worming her way through keyholes and listening to people's secrets, or hitching a free lift round the houses in her enemy the postman's pocket and jabbing him with a darning needle as a reward for the ride, or sculling about the pond on Farmer Beezeley's ducks and driving them frantic by tickling them under their wings, or galloping down the street on somebody's furious collie, or climbing into the vicar's TV and frightening him half to death by shouting "Time is short!" through the screen. She frequently ran fearful risks but seemed to have a charmed life. Everybody in the village heartily detested Min Perrow, but her elder brothers and sisters were devoted to her and rather proud of her exploits.

Poor Dizzry continued to cry, on and off, for the rest of the day. Harriet tried to console her but it seemed horribly probable that Min had at last gone too far and had been swallowed by a cow or drowned in a sump or rolled into a Swiss roll at the bakery while stealing jam – so many ill fates might easily have befallen her that it was hard to guess the likeliest.

"I'll help you hunt for her this evening," Harriet promised, however, "and so will Mark. As soon as my birthday tea's finished."

Dizzry came home with Harriet for the birthday tea and was a little cheered by the cake made in the shape of a penguin with blackcurrant icing and an orange beak, and Harriet's presents, which included a do-it-yourself water-divining kit from Mark (a hazel twig and a bucket of water), an electronic guitar which could sing as well as play, a little pocket computer for working out sums and, from Harriet's fairy godmother, a tube of everlasting toothpaste. Harriet was not particularly grateful for this last; the thought of toothpaste supplied for the rest of her life left her unmoved.

"I'd rather have had an endless stick of liquorice," she said crossly. "Probably I shan't have any teeth left by the time I'm ninety; what use will toothpaste be then?"

Her presents from Dizzry were by far the nicest: a pink and orange necklace of spindleberries, beautifully carved, and a starling named Alastair whom Dizzry had trained to take messages, answer the telephone or the front door, and carry home small quantities of shopping.

"Now," said Mrs Armitage rather nervously when the

presents had been admired, "I'd better show Harriet the Closed Room."

Mr Armitage hurriedly retired to his study while Mark, controlling some natural feelings of envy, kindly said he would help Dizzry hunt for Min, and carried her off to inspect all the reapers and binders in Mr Beezeley's farmyard.

Harriet and Mrs Armitage went up to the attic floor and Mrs Armitage paused before a cobweb-shrouded door and pulled a rusty old key out of her pocket.

"Now you must say 'I, Harriet Armitage, solemnly swear not to reveal the secret of this room to any other soul in the world.'"

"But when I grow up and have a daughter," objected Harriet, "won't I have to tell her, just as Granny told you and you're telling me?"

"Well, yes, I suppose so," Mrs Armitage said uncertainly. "I've rather forgotten how the oath went, to tell you the truth."

"Why do we have to promise not to tell?"

"To be honest, I haven't the faintest idea."

"Let's skip that bit — there doesn't seem much point to it — and just go in," Harriet suggested. So they opened the door (it was very stiff, for it had been shut at least twenty years) and went in.

The attic was dim, lit only by a patch of green glass tiles in the roof; it was quite empty except for a small, dusty loom, made of black wood, with a stool to match.

"A loom?" said Harriet, very disappointed. "Is *that* all?"

"It isn't an ordinary loom," her mother corrected her. "It's a hairloom. For weaving human hair."

"Who wants to weave human hair? What can you make?"

"I suppose you make a human hair mat. You must only use hair that's never been cut since birth."

"Haven't you ever tried?"

"Oh my dear, I never seemed to get a chance. When I was your age and Granny first showed me the loom everyone wore their hair short; you couldn't get a bit long enough to weave for love or money. And then you children came along – somehow I never found time."

"Well I jolly well shall," Harriet said. "I'll try and get hold of some hair. I wonder if Miss Pring would let me have hers? I bet it's never been cut – she must have yards. Maybe you can make a cloak of invisibility, or the sort that turns swans into humans."

She was so pleased with this notion that only as they went downstairs did she think to ask, "How did the loom get into the family?"

"I'm a bit vague about that," Mrs Armitage admitted. "I believe it belonged to a Greek ancestress that one of the crusading Armitages married and brought back to England. She's the one I'm called Penelope after."

Without paying much attention, Harriet went off to find Mark and Dizzry. Her father said they were along at the church, so she followed, pausing at the post office to ask elderly Miss Pring the postmistress if she would sell her long grey hair to be woven into a rug.

"It would look very pretty," she coaxed. "I could dye some of it pink or blue."

Miss Pring was not keen.

"Sell my hair? Cut it off? The idea! *Dye* it? What impertinence! Get along with you, sauce-box!"

So Harriet had to abandon that scheme, but she stuck up a postcard on the notice-board: HUMAN HAIR REQUIRED, UNCUT; BEST PRICES PAID, and posted off another to the local paper. Then she joined Mark and Dizzry, who were searching the church organ pipes, but without success.

Harriet had met several other members of the Perrow family on her way: Ernie, Min's father, driving an old dolls' push-chair which he had fitted with an engine and turned into a convertible like a Model T Ford; old Gran Perrow, stomping along and gloomily shouting "Min!" down all the drain-holes; and Sid, one of the boys, riding a bike made from cocoa tins and poking out nests from the hedge with a bamboo in case Min had been abducted.

When it was too dark to go on searching Harriet and Mark left Dizzry at Rose Cottage, where the Perrows lived.

"We'll go on looking tomorrow!" they called. And Harriet said, "Don't worry too much."

"I expect she'll be all right wherever she is," Mark said. "I'd back Min against a mad bull any day."

As they walked home he asked Harriet:

"What about the Closed Room, then? Any monster?"

"No, very dull – just a hairloom."

"I say, you shouldn't tell me, should you?"

"It's all right — we agreed to skip the promise to keep it secret."

"What a let-down," Mark said. "Who wants an old loom?"

They arrived home to trouble. Their father was complaining, as he did every day, about soot on the carpets and black tide-marks on the bathroom basin and towels.

"Well, if you don't *want* me to find Lady Anne's necklace..." Mark said aggrievedly. "If it was worth a thousand pounds when she lost it in 1660, think what it would fetch now."

"Why in heaven's name would it be up the *chimney*? Stop arguing and go to bed. And brush your teeth!"

"I'll lend you some of my toothpaste," Harriet said.

"Just the same," Mark grumbled, brushing his teeth with yards of toothpaste so that the foam stood out on either side of his face like Dundreary whiskers and flew all over the bathroom, "Ernie Perrow definitely told me that his great-great-great-grandfather Oliver Perrow had a row with Lady Anne Armitage because she ticked him off for catching field-mice in her orchard; Oliver was the village sweep, and her pearls vanished just after; Ernie thinks old Oliver stuck them in the chimney to teach her a lesson, and then he died, eaten by a fox before he had a chance to tell anyone. But Ernie's sure that's where the pearls are."

"Perhaps Min's up there looking for them too."

"Not her! She'd never do anything as useful as that."

Harriet had asked Alastair the starling to call her at

seven; in fact she was roused at half past six by loud bangs on the front door.

"For heaven's sake, somebody, tell that maniac to go away!" shouted Mr Armitage from under his pillow.

Harriet flung on a dressing-gown and ran downstairs. What was her surprise to find at the door a little old man in a white duffel-coat with the hood up. He carried a very large parcel, wrapped in sacking. Harriet found the sharp look he gave her curiously disconcerting.

"Would it be Miss Armitage now, the young lady who put the advertisement in the paper then?"

"About hair?" Harriet said eagerly. "Yes, I did. Have you got some, Mr...?"

"Mr Thomas Jones, the Druid, I am. Beautiful hair I have then, look you – finer than any lady's in the land. Only see now till I get this old parcel undone!" And he dumped the bundle down at her feet and started unknotting the cords. Harriet helped. When the last half-hitch twanged apart a great springy mass of hair came boiling out. It was soft and fine, dazzlingly white with just a few strands of black, and smelt slightly of tobacco.

"There, now indeed to goodness! Did you ever see finer?"

"But," said Harriet, "has it ever been cut short?" She very much hoped that it had not; it seemed impossible that they would ever be able to parcel it up again.

"Never has a scissor-blade been laid to it, till I cut it all off last night," the old man declared.

Harriet wondered whose it was; something slightly malicious and self-satisfied about the old man's grin as he said "I cut it all off" prevented her from asking.

"Er – how much would you want for it?" she inquired cautiously.

"Well indeed," he said. "It would be hard to put a price on such beautiful hair, whatever."

At this moment there came an interruption. A large van drew up in front of the Armitage house. On its sides iridescent bubbles were painted, and, in rainbow colours, the words SUGDEN'S SOAP.

A uniformed driver jumped out, consulting a piece of paper.

"Mr Mark Armitage live here?" he asked Harriet. She nodded.

"Will he take delivery of one bathroom, complete with shower, tub, footbath, de-luxe basin, plastic curtains, turkish towelling, chrome sponge-holder, steel and enamel hair drier, and a six years' supply of Sugden's Soap?"

"I suppose so," Harriet said doubtfully. "You're sure there's no mistake?"

The delivery note certainly had Mark's name and address.

"Mark!" Harriet yelled up the stairs, forgetting it was still only seven a.m. "Did you order a bathroom? Because it's come."

"Merciful goodness!" groaned the voice of Mr Armitage. "Has *no* one any consideration for my hours of rest?"

Mark came running down, looking slightly embarrassed.

"Darn it," he said as he signed the delivery note, "I never expected I'd get a *bathroom*; I was hoping for the free cruise to Saposoa."

"Where shall we put it, guv?" said the driver, who was plainly longing to be away and get some breakfast at the nearest carmen's pull-in.

Mark looked about him vaguely. At this moment Mr Armitage came downstairs in pyjamas and a very troublesome frame of mind.

"Bathroom? Bathroom?" he said. "You've bought a bathroom? What the blazes did you want to go and get a bathroom for? Isn't the one we have good enough for you, pray? You leave it dirty enough. Who's going to pay for this? And why has nobody put the kettle on?"

"I won it," Mark explained, blushing. "It was the second prize in the Sugden's Soap competition. In the *Radio Times*, you know."

"What did you have to do?" Harriet asked.

"Ten uses for soap in correct order of importance."

"I bet *washing* came right at the bottom," growled his father. "Greased stairs and fake soft-centres are more your mark."

"Anyway he won!" Harriet pointed out. "Was that all you had to do?"

"You had to write a couplet too."

"What was yours?"

Mark blushed even pinker. "Rose or White or Heliotrope, Where there's life there's Sugden's Soap."

"Come on now," said the van driver patiently, "we don't want to be here all day, do we? Where shall we put it, guv? In the garden?"

"Certainly not," snapped Mr Armitage. He was proud of his garden.

"How about in the field?" suggested Harriet diplomatically. "Then Mark and I can wash in it, and you needn't be upset by soot on the towels."

"That's true," her father said, brightening a little. "All right, stick it in the field. And now will somebody *please* put on a kettle and make a cup of tea, is that too much to ask?" And he stomped back to bed, leaving Mark and the driver to organize the erection of the bathroom in the field beside the house. Harriet put a kettle on the stove and went back to Mr Jones the Druid who was sunning himself in the front porch.

"Have you decided what you want for your hair?" she asked.

"Oh," he said. "There is a grand new bathroom you have with you! Lucky that is, indeed. Now I am thinking I do not want any money at all for my fine bundle of hair, but only to strike a bargain with you."

"Very well," Harriet said cautiously.

"No bathroom I have at my place, see? Hard it is to wash the old beard, and chilly of a winter morning in the stream. But if you and your brother, that I can see is a kind-hearted obliging young gentleman, would let me come and give it a bit of a lather now and again in *your* bathroom…"

"Why yes, of course," Harriet said. "I'm sure Mark won't mind at all."

"So it shall be, then. Handy that will be, indeed. Terrible deal of the old beard there is, look you, and grubby she do get."

With that he undid his duffel-coat and pulled back the hood. All round his head and wound about his body like an Indian sari was a prodigiously long white beard which he proceeded to untwine until it trailed on the ground. It was similar to the white hair in the bundle, but not so clean.

"Is that somebody's beard, then?" Harriet asked, pointing to the bundle.

"My twin brother, Dai Jones the Bard. Bathroom he has by him, the lucky old *cythryblwr*! But soon I will be getting a bigger one. Made a will, my Dad did, see, leaving all his money to the one of us who has the longest and whitest beard on our ninetieth birthday, that falls tomorrow on Midsummer Day. So I crept into his house last night and cut his beard off while he slept; hard he'll find it now to grow another beard in time! All Dada's money I will be getting, he, he, he!"

Mr Jones the Druid chuckled maliciously.

Harriet could not help thinking he was rather a wicked old man, but a bargain was a bargain, so she picked up the bundle of beard, with difficulty, and was about to say goodbye when he stopped her.

"Weaving the hair into a mat, you would be, isn't it?" he said wheedlingly. "There is a fine bath-mat it would make! Towels and curtains there are in that grand new bathroom of yours but no bath-mat – pity that is, indeed." He gave her a cunning look out of the corners of his eyes, but Harriet would not commit herself.

"Come along this evening, then, I will, for a good old wash-up before my birthday," Mr Jones said. He wound himself in his beard again and went off with many nods and bows. Harriet ran to the field to see how the bathroom was getting on. Mark had it nearly finished. True enough, there was no bath-mat. It struck Harriet that Mr Jones's suggestion was not a bad one.

"I'll start weaving a mat as soon as we've had another thorough hunt for Min Perrow," she said. "Saturday, thank goodness, no school."

However during breakfast (which was late, owing to these various events) Ernie Perrow drove along in the push-chair with Lily and Dizzry to show the Armitages an air letter which had arrived from the British Consul in Cathay.

Dear Sir or Madam,
    Kindly make earliest arrangements to send
passage money back to England for your
daughter Hermione who has had herself posted
here, stowed away in a box of Health Biscuits.
Please forward without delay fare and expenses
totalling £1,093 7s. 1d.

A postscript, scrawled by Min, read: 'Dun it at larst! Sux to silly old postmun!'

"Oh, what shall we do?" wept Mrs Perrow. "A thousand pounds! How can we ever find it?"

While the grown-ups discussed ways and means, Mark went back to his daily search for Lady Anne's pearls, and Harriet took the woebegone Dizzry up to the attic, hoping to distract her by a look at the hairloom.

Dizzry was delighted with it. "Do let's do some weaving!" she said. "I like weaving better than anything."

So Harriet lugged in the great bundle of beard and they set up the loom. Dizzry was an expert weaver. She had been making beautiful scarves for years on a child's toy loom – she could nip to and fro with the shuttle almost faster than Harriet's eyes could follow. By tea-time they had woven a handsome thick white mat with the words bath ma across the middle (there had not been quite enough black for the final T).

"Anyway you can see what it's meant to be," Harriet said. They took the new mat and spread it in their elegant bathroom.

"Tell you what," Mark said, "we'd better hide the bath and basin plugs when Min gets back or she'll climb in and drown herself."

"Oh, I do wonder what Dad and Mum are doing about getting her back," sighed Dizzry, who was sitting on a sponge. She wiped her eyes on a corner of Harriet's face-cloth.

"Let's go along to your house," Harriet said, "and find out."

There was an atmosphere of deep gloom in the Perrow

household. Ernie had arranged to sell his Model T push-chair, the apple of his eye, to the Motor Museum at Beaulieu.

"A thousand pound they say they'll give for it," he said miserably. "With that and what I've saved from the chimney sweeping, we can just about pay the fare. Won't I half clobber young Min when I get her back, the little varmint!"

"Mrs Perrow," Harriet said, "may Dizzry come and spend the evening at our house, as Mother and Daddy are going to a dance? And have a bath in our new bathroom? Mother says it's all right and I'll take great care of her."

"Oh, very well, if your Ma doesn't mind," sighed Mrs Perrow. "I'm so distracted I hardly know if I'm coming or going. Don't forget your wash things, Diz, and the bath-salts."

Harriet was enchanted with the bath-salts, no bigger than hundreds-and-thousands.

On Midsummer Eve the Armitage children were allowed to stay up as late as they liked. Mark, a single-minded boy, said he intended to go on hunting for Lady Anne's necklace in the chimney. The girls had their baths and then went up to Harriet's room with a bagful of apples and the gramophone, intending to have a good gossip.

At half past eleven Harriet, happening to glance out of the window, saw a light in the field.

"That must be Mr Jones," she said. "I'd forgotten he was coming to shampoo his beard. It's not Mark, I can still hear him bumping around in the chimney."

There was indeed an excited banging to be heard from the chimney-breast, but it was as nothing compared with the terrible racket that suddenly broke out in the field. They heard shouts and cries of rage, thuds, crashes, and the tinkle of smashed glass.

"Heavens, what can be going on?" cried Harriet. She flung up the sash and prepared to climb out of the window.

"Wait for me!" said Dizzry.

"Here, jump into my pocket. Hold tight!"

Harriet slid down the wisteria and dashed across the garden. A moment later they arrived at the bathroom door and witnessed a wild scene.

Evidently Mr Jones the Druid had finished washing his beard and been about to leave when he saw his doom waiting for him outside the door in the form of another, very angry, old man who was trying to batter his way in.

"It must be his brother!" Harriet whispered. "Mr Jones the Bard!"

The second old man had no beard, only a ragged white frill cut short round his chin. He was shouting,

"Wait till I catch you, you *hocsdwr*, you *herwhaliwr*, you *ffrawddunio*, you wicked old *llechwr*! A snake would think shame to spit on you! Cutting off your brother's beard, indeed! Just let me get at you and I'll trim you to spillikins. I'll shave your beard round your eyebrows!" And he beat on the door with a huge pair of shears. A pane of glass fell in and broke on the bathroom tiles; then the whole door gave way.

Dizzry left Harriet's pocket and swarmed up on to her head to see what was happening. They heard a fearful bellow from inside the bathroom, a stamping and crashing, fierce grunts, the hiss of the shower and more breaking glass.

"Hey!" Harriet shouted. "Stop wrecking our bathroom!"

No answer. The noise of battle went on.

Then the bathroom window flew open and Jones the Druid shot out, all tangled in his beard which was snowy white now, but still damp. He had the bath-mat rolled up under his arm. As soon as he was out he flung it down, leapt on it, and shouted, "Take me out of here!"

The mat took off vertically and hovered, about seven feet up, while Mr Jones began hauling in his damp beard, hand over hand.

"Come back!" Harriet cried. "You've no right to go off with our bath-mat."

Jones the Bard came roaring out of the window, waving his shears.

"Come back, *ystraffaldiach*! Will you come down off there and let me mince you into macaroni! Oh, you wicked old weasel, I'll trim your beard shorter than an earwig's toe-nails!"

He made a grab for the bath-mat but it was just out of reach.

"He, he, he!" cackled Jones the Druid up above. "You didn't know your fine beard would make up so nice into a flying carpet, did you, brother? Has to be woven on a hairloom on Midsummer Eve and then it'll carry you faster than the Aberdovey Flyer."

"Just let me get at you, *rheibiwr!*" snarled Jones the Bard, making another vain grab.

But Dizzry, who was now jumping up and down on the top of Harriet's head, made a tremendous spring, grabbed hold of a trailing strand of Mr Jones's beard, and hauled herself up on to a corner of the flying bath-mat.

"Oh dammo!" gasped the Druid at sight of her. He was so taken aback that he lost his balance, staggered, and fell headlong on top of his brother. There was a windmill confusion of arms and legs, all swamped by the foaming mass of beard. Then Jones the Bard grabbed his shears with a shout of triumph and began chopping away great swags of white hair.

Harriet, however, paid no heed to these goings-on.

"*Dizzry!*" she shouted, cupping her hands round her mouth. "It's a wishing-mat. Make it take you—"

Dizzry nodded. She needed no telling. "Take me to Cathay!" she cried, and the mat soared away through the milky air of midsummer night.

At this moment Mark came running across the field.

"Oh, Mark!" Harriet burst out. "Look what those old fiends have done to our bathroom! It's ruined. They ought to be made to pay for it."

Mark glanced through the broken window. The place was certainly a shambles: bath and basin were both smashed, the sponge-rack was wrapped round the hair-drier, the towels were trodden into a soggy pulp and the curtains were in ribbons.

The Jones brothers were in equally bad shape. Jones the Bard was kneeling on Jones the Druid's stomach; he had managed to trim every shred of hair off his brother's head, but he himself was as bald as a coot. Both had black eyes and swollen lips.

"Oh well," Mark said. "They seem to have trouble of their own. I bet neither of them comes into that legacy now. And I never did care much for washing anyway. Look, here comes Dizzry back."

The bath-mat swooped to a three-point landing, Dizzry and Min rolled off it, laughing and crying.

"You wicked, wicked, bad little girl," Dizzry cried, shaking and hugging her small sister at the same time. "Don't you ever dare do such a thing again!"

"Now I will take my own property which is my lawful beard," said Mr Jones the Bard, and he jumped off his brother's stomach on to the mat and addressed it in a flood of Welsh, which it evidently understood, for it rose into the air and flew off in a westerly direction. Mr Jones the Druid slunk away across the field looking, Dizzry said, as hangdog as a cat that has fallen into the milk.

"Now we've lost our bath-mat," Harriet sighed.

"I'll help you make another," Dizzry said. "There's plenty of hair lying about. And at least we've got Min back."

"Was it nice in Cathay, Min?" Mark said.

"Smashing. I had rice-cake and cherry ice and Coca-Cola."

At this point Mr and Mrs Armitage returned from their

dance and kindly drove Dizzry and Min home to break the joyful news to their parents.

Harriet and Mark had a try at putting the bathroom to rights, but it was really past hope.

"I must say, trouble certainly haunts this household," remarked Mr Armitage, when he came back and found them at it. "Hurry up and get to bed, you two. Do you realize it's four o'clock on midsummer morning? Oh, Lord, I suppose now we have to go back to the old regime of sooty footmarks all over the bathroom."

"Certainly not," said Mark. "I'd forgotten to tell you. I found Lady Anne's pearls."

He pulled them out and dangled them: a soot-black, six-foot double strand of pearls as big as cobnuts, probably worth a king's ransom.

"Won't Ernie Perrow be pleased to know they really were in the chimney?" he said.

"Oh, get to bed!" snapped his father. "I'm fed up with hearing about the Perrows."

Eleven

A Leg Full of Rubies

Night, now. And a young man, Theseus O'Brien, coming down the main street of Killinch with an owl seated upon his shoulder – perhaps the strangest sight that small town ever witnessed. The high moors brooded around the town, all up the wide street came the sighing of the river, and the August night was as gentle and full as a bucket of new milk.

Theseus turned into Tom Mahone's snug, where the men of the town were gathered peaceably together, breathing smoke and drinking mountain dew. Wild, he seemed, coming into the lamplit circle, with a look of the night on him, and a small of loneliness about him, and his eyes had an inward glimmer from looking into the dark. The owl on his shoulder sat quiet as a coffee-pot.

"Well, now, God be good to ye," said Tom Mahone. "What can we do for ye at all?"

And he poured a strong drop, to warm the four bones of him.

"Is there a veterinary surgeon in this town?" Theseus inquired.

Then they saw that the owl had a hurt wing, the ruffled feathers all at odds with one another. "Is there a man in this town can mend him?" he said.

"Ah, sure Dr Kilvaney's the man for ye," said they all. "No less than a magician with the sick beasts, he is." "And can throw a boulder farther than any man in the land." "'Tis the same one has a wooden leg stuffed full of rubies." "And keeps a phoenix in a cage." "And has all the minutes of his life numbered to the final grain of sand — ah, he's the man to aid ye."

And all the while the owl staring at them from great round eyes.

No more than a step it was to the Doctor's surgery, with half Tom Mahone's customers pointing the way. The Doctor, sitting late to his supper by a small black fire, heard the knock and opened the door, candle in hand.

"Hoo?" said the owl at sight of him, "who, whoo?" And, *who* indeed may this strange man be, thought Theseus, following him down the stone passageway, with his long white hair and his burning eyes of grief?

Not a word was said between them till the owl's wing was set, and then the Doctor, seeing O'Brien was weary, made him sit and drink a glass of wine.

"Sit," said he, "there's words to be spoken between us. How long has the owl belonged to you?"

"To me?" said Theseus. "He's no owl of mine. I found him up on the high moor. Can you mend him?"

"He'll be well in three days," said Kilvaney. "I see you are a man after my heart, with a love of wild creatures. Are you not a doctor, too?"

"I am," answered Theseus. "Or I was," he added sadly, "until the troubles of my patients became too great a grief for me to bear, and I took to walking the roads to rid me of it."

"Come into my surgery," said the Doctor, "for I've things to show you. You're the man I've been looking for."

They passed through the kitchen, where a girl was washing the dishes. Lake-blue eyes, she had, and black hair; she was small, and fierce, and beautiful, like a falcon.

"My daughter," the Doctor said absently. "Go to bed, Maggie."

"When the birds are fed, not before," she snapped.

Cage after cage of birds, Theseus saw, all down one wall of the room, finches and thrushes, starlings and blackbirds, with a sleepy stirring and twittering coming from them.

In the surgery there was only one cage, but that one big enough to house a man. And inside it was such a bird as Theseus had never seen before – every feather on it pure gold, and eyes like candle-flames.

"My phoenix," the Doctor said, "but don't go too near him, for he's vicious."

The phoenix sidled near the end of the cage, with his eyes full of malice and his wicked beak sideways, ready to strike. Theseus stepped away from the cage and saw, at the other end of the room, a mighty hour-glass that held in its twin globes enough sand to boil all the eggs in Leghorn. But most of the sand had run through, and only a thin stream remained, silting down so swiftly on the pyramid below that every minute Theseus expected to see the last grain whirl through and vanish.

"You are only just in time," Dr Kilvaney said. "My hour has come. I hereby appoint you my heir and successor. To you I bequeath my birds. Feed them well, treat them kindly, and they will sing to you. But never, never let the phoenix out of his cage, for his nature is evil."

"No, no! Dr Kilvaney!" Theseus cried. "You are in the wrong of it! You are putting a terrible thing on me! I don't want your birds, not a feather of them. I can't abide creatures in cages!"

"You must have them," said the Doctor coldly. "Who else can I trust? And to you I leave also my wooden leg full of rubies – look, I will show you how it unscrews."

"No!" cried Theseus. "I don't want to see!"

He shut his eyes, but he heard a creaking, like a wooden pump-handle.

"And I will give you, too," said the Doctor presently, "this hour-glass. See, my last grain of sand has run through. Now it will be *your* turn." Calmly he reversed the hour-glass, and started the sand once more on its silent, hurrying journey. Then he said:

"Surgery hours are on the board outside. The medicines

are in the cupboard yonder. Bridget Hanlon is the midwife. My daughter feeds the birds and attends to the cooking. You can sleep tonight on the bed in here. Never let the phoenix out of its cage. You must promise that."

"I promise," said Theseus, like a dazed man.

"Now I will say goodbye to you." The Doctor took out his false teeth, put them on the table, glanced round the room to see that nothing was overlooked, and then went up the stairs as if he were late for an appointment.

All night Theseus, uneasy on the surgery couch, could hear the whisper of the sand running, and the phoenix rustling, and the whet of its beak on the bars; with the first light he could see its mad eye glaring at him.

In the morning Doctor Kilvaney was dead.

It was a grand funeral. All the town gathered to pay him respect, for he had dosed and drenched and bandaged them all, and brought most of them into the world, too.

" 'Tis a sad loss," said Tom Mahone, "and he with the grandest collection of cage-birds this side of Dublin city. 'Twas in a happy hour for us the young doctor turned up to take his place."

But there was no happiness in the heart of Theseus O'Brien. Like a wild thing caged himself he felt, among the rustling birds, and with the hating eye of the phoenix fixing him from its corner, and, worst of all, the steady fall of sand from the hour-glass to drive him half mad with its whispering threat.

And, to add to his troubles, no sooner were they home

from the funeral than Maggie packed up her clothes in a carpet-bag and moved to the other end of the town to live with her aunt Rose, who owned the hay and feed store.

"It wouldn't be decent," said she, "to keep house for you, and you a single man." And the more Theseus pleaded, the firmer and fiercer she grew. "Besides," she said, "I wouldn't live another day among all those poor birds behind bars. I can't stand the sight nor sound of them."

"I'll let them go, Maggie! I'll let every one of them go."

But then he remembered, with a falling heart, the Doctor's last command. "That is, all except the phoenix."

Maggie turned away. All down the village street he watched her small, proud back, until she crossed the bridge and was out of sight. And it seemed as if his heart went with her.

The very next day he let loose all the Doctor's birds – the finches and thrushes, the starlings and blackbirds, the woodpecker and the wild heron. He thought Maggie looked at him with a kinder eye when he walked up to the hay and feed store to tell her what he had done.

The people of the town grew fond of their new doctor, but they lamented his sad and downcast look. "What ails him at all?" they asked one another, and Tom Mahone said, "He's as mournful as old Doctor Kilvaney was before him. Sure there's something insalubrious about carrying on the profession of medicine in this town."

But indeed, it was not his calling that troubled the poor young man, for here his patients were as carefree a set of citizens as he could wish. It was the ceaseless running of the sand.

Although there was a whole roomful of sand to run through the glass, he couldn't stop thinking of the day when that roomful would be dwindled to a mere basketful, and then to nothing but a bowlful. And the thought dwelt on his mind like a blight, since it is not wholesome for a man to be advised when his latter end will come, no matter what the burial service may say.

Not only the sand haunted him, but also the phoenix, with its unrelenting state of hate. No matter what delicacies he brought it, in the way of bird-seed and kibbled corn, dry mash and the very best granite grit (for his visits to the hay and feed store were the high spot of his days) the phoenix was always waiting with its razor-sharp beak ready to lay him open to the bone should he venture too near. None of the food would it more than nibble at. And a thing he began to notice, as the days went past, was that its savage brooding eye was always focused on one part of his anatomy – on his left leg. It sometimes seemed to him as if the bird had a particular stake or claim to that leg, and meant to keep watch and see that its property was maintained in good condition.

One night Theseus had need of a splint for a patient. He reached up to a high shelf, where he kept the mastoid mallets, and the crutches, and surgical chisels. He was standing on a chair to do it, and suddenly his foot slipped and he fell, bringing down with him a mighty bone-saw that came to the ground beside him with a clang and a twang, missing his left knee-cap by something less than a feather's breadth. Pale and shaken, he got up, and turning, saw the phoenix watching him as usual, but with such an intent and disappointed look, like the housewife who sees the butcher's boy approaching with the wrong joint!

A cold fit of shivering came over Theseus, and he went hurriedly out of the room.

Next day when he was returning home over the bridge, carrying a bag full of bird-mash, with dried milk and antibiotics added, and his mind full of the blue eyes and black hair of Maggie, a runaway tractor hurtled past him and crashed into the parapet, only one centimetre beyond his left foot.

And again Theseus shuddered, and walked home white and silent, with the cold thought on him. He found the phoenix hunched on its perch, feathers up and head sunk.

"Ah, Phoenix, Phoenix," he cried to it, "why will you be persecuting me so? Do you want to destroy me entirely?" The phoenix made no reply, but stared balefully at his left leg. Then he remembered the old Doctor's wooden leg full of rubies. "But I'll not wear it!" he cried to the bird, "not if it was stuffed with rubies and diamonds too!"

Just the same, in his heart he believed that the phoenix would not rest satisfied while he had the use of both his legs. He took to walking softly, like a cat, looking this way and that for all possible hazards, watching for falling tiles, and boiling saucepans, and galloping cattle; and the people of the town began to shake their heads over him.

His only happy hours were with Maggie, when he could persuade her to leave the store and come out walking with him. Far out of the town they'd go, forgetting the troubles that lay at home. For Maggie had found her aunt was a small, mean-minded woman who put sand in with the hens' meal and shingle among the maize, and Maggie couldn't abide such dealings.

"As soon as I've a little saved," said she, "I'll be away from this town, and off into the world."

"Maggie!" cried Theseus, and it was the first time he'd plucked up courage to do so. "Marry me, and I'll make you happier than any girl in the length and breadth of this land."

"I can't marry you," she said. "I could never, never marry a man who kept a phoenix in a cage."

"We'll give it away," he said, "give it away and forget about it." But even as he spoke he knew they could not. They kissed despairingly, up on the moors in the twilight, and turned homewards.

"I always knew that phoenix was a trouble-bringer," said Maggie, "from the day when Father bought it off a travelling tinker to add to his collection. He said at the time it was a bargain, for the tinker threw in the wooden leg and the great hour-glass as well, but ever after that day Father was a changed man."

"What did he give for it?" Theseus asked.

"His peace of mind. That was all the tinker asked, but it

was a deal too much, I'm thinking, for that hateful bird with his wicked look and his revengeful ways."

When he had seen Maggie home, Theseus went to the Public Library, for he couldn't abide the thought of the Doctor's house, dark and cold and silent with only the noise of the phoenix shifting on its perch. He took down the volume OWL to POL of the encyclopedia and sat studying it until closing time.

Next day he was along to see Maggie.

"Sweetheart," he said, and his eyes were alive with hope, "I believe I've found the answer. Let me have a half-hundredweight sack of layers' pellets."

"Fourteen shillings," snapped Aunt Rose, who happened to be in the shop just then. Her hair was pinned up in a skinny bun and her little green eyes were like brad-awls.

"Discount for cash payment," snapped back Theseus, and he planked down thirteen shillings and ninepence, kissed Maggie, picked up the sack, and hurried away home. Just as he got there a flying slate from the church roof struck him; if he'd not been wearing heavy boots it would have sliced his foot off. He ran indoors and shook his fist at the phoenix.

"There!" he yelled at it, pouring a troughful of layers' pellets. "Now get that in your gizzard, you misbegotten fowl!"

The phoenix cocked its head. Then it pecked a pellet, neck feathers puffed in scorn, and one satiric eye fixed all the while on Theseus, who stood eagerly watching. Then it pecked another pellet, hanging by one claw from its perch. Then it came down on to the floor entirely and bowed its golden head over the trough. Theseus tiptoed out of the room. He went outside and chopped up a few sticks of kindling – not many, but just a handful of nice, dry, thin twigs. He came back indoors – the phoenix had its head down, gobbling – and laid the sticks alongside the cage, not too close, an artful width away.

Next evening, surgery done, he fairly ran up to the hay and feed store. "Come with me," he said joyfully to Maggie, "come and see what it's doing."

Maggie came, her eyes blazing with curiosity. When they reached the surgery she could hear a crackling and a cracking: the phoenix was breaking up twigs into suitable lengths, and laying them side by side. Every now and then it would try them out in a heap; it had a great bundle in the bottom of its cage but it seemed dissatisfied, and every now and then pulled it all to pieces and began again. It had eaten the whole sackful of pellets and looked plump and sleek.

"Theseus," said Maggie, looking at it, "we must let it out. No bird can build inside of a cage. It's not dignified."

"But my promise?"

"*I* never promised," said Maggie, and she stepped up to the cage door.

Theseus lifted a hand, opened his mouth in warning. But then he stopped. For the phoenix, when it saw what Maggie was at, inclined its head to her in gracious acknowledgement, and then took no further notice of her, but, as soon as the door was opened, began shifting its heap of sticks out into the room. If ever a bird was busy and preoccupied and in a hurry, that phoenix was the one.

"But we can't let it build in the middle of the floor," said Theseus.

"Ah, sure, what harm?" said Maggie. "Look, the poor fowl is running short of sticks."

As soon as Theseus had gone for more, she stepped over to the hour-glass, for her quick eye had noticed what he, in his excitement, had failed to see – the sand was nearly all run through. Quietly, Maggie reversed the glass and started the sand on its journey again, a thing she had often done for her father, unbeknownst, until the day when it was plain he would rather die than stay alive.

When Theseus came back the phoenix was sitting proudly on the top of a breast-high heap of sticks.

"We mustn't watch it now," said Maggie, "it wouldn't be courteous." And she led Theseus outside. He, however, could not resist a slant-eyed glance through the window as they passed. It yielded him a flash of gold – the phoenix had laid an egg in a kidney-basin. Moreover, plumes of smoke were beginning to flow out through the window.

"Goodbye, phoenix," Maggie called. But the phoenix, at the heart of a golden blaze, was much too busy to reply.

"Thank heaven!" exclaimed Theseus. "Now I shall never know when the last of my sand was due to run through." Maggie smiled, but made no comment, and he asked her, "Is it right, do you think, to let the house burn down?"

"What harm?" said Maggie again. "It belongs to us, doesn't it?"

"What will the people of the town do, if I'm not here to doctor them?"

"Go to Doctor Conlan of Drumanough."

"And what about your father's leg full of rubies?" he said, looking at the phoenix's roaring pyre.

"We'd never get it out now," said she. "Let it go on holding up the kitchen table till they both burn. We've better things to think of."

And hand in hand the happy pair of them ran out of the town, up along the road to the high moors and the world, leaving behind a pocketful of rubies to glitter in the ashes, and a golden egg for anyone who was fool enough to pick it up.

Twelve

THE SERIAL GARDEN

"COLD RICE PUDDING for breakfast?" said Mark, looking at it with disfavour.

"Don't be fussy," said his mother. "You're the only one who's complaining." This was unfair, for she and Mark were the only members of the family at table, Harriet having developed measles while staying with a school friend, while Mr Armitage had somehow managed to lock himself in the larder. Mrs Armitage never had anything but toast and marmalade for breakfast anyway.

Mark went on scowling at the chilly-looking pudding. It had come straight out of the fridge, which was not in the larder.

"If you don't like it," said Mrs Armitage, "unless you want Daddy to pass you cornflakes through the larder ventilator, flake by flake, you'd better run down to Miss Pride and get a small packet of cereal. She opens at eight; Hickmans don't open till nine. It's no use waiting till the blacksmith comes to let your father out; I'm sure he won't be here for hours yet."

There came a gloomy banging from the direction of the larder, just to remind them that Mr Armitage was alive and suffering in there.

"*You're* all right," shouted Mark heartlessly as he passed the larder door, "there's nothing to stop you having cornflakes. Oh I forgot, the milk's in the fridge. Well, have cheese and pickles then. Or treacle tart."

Even through the zinc grating on the door he could hear his father shudder at the thought of treacle tart and pickles for breakfast. Mr Armitage's imprisonment was his own fault, though; he had sworn that he was going to find out where the mouse got into the larder if it took him all night, watching and waiting. He had shut himself in, so that no member of the family should come bursting in and disturb his vigil. The larder door had a spring catch, which sometimes jammed; it was bad luck that this turned out to be one of the times.

Mark ran across the fields to Miss Pride's shop at Sticks Corner and asked if she had any cornflakes.

"Oh, I don't think I have any left, dear," Miss Pride said woefully. "I'll have a look… I think I sold the last packet a week ago Tuesday."

"What about the one in the window?"

"That's a dummy, dear."

Miss Pride's shop-window was full of nasty old cardboard cartons with nothing inside them, and several empty display stands which had fallen down and never been propped up again. Inside the shop were a few small tired-looking tins and jars, which had a worn and scratched appearance as if mice had tried them and given up. Miss Pride herself was small and wan, with yellowish grey hair; she rooted rather hopelessly in a pile of empty boxes. Mark's mother never bought any groceries from Miss Pride if she could help it, since the day when she had found a label inside the foil wrapping of a cream cheese saying 'This cheese should be eaten before May 11th, 1899'.

"No cornflakes, I'm afraid, dear."

"Any Wheat Crispies? Puffed Corn? Rice Nuts?"

"No, dear. Nothing left, only Brekkfast Brikks."

"Never heard of *them*," said Mark doubtfully.

"Or I've a jar of Ovo here. You spread it on bread. That's nice for breakfast," said Miss Pride with a sudden burst of salesmanship. Mark thought the Ovo looked beastly, like yellow paint, so he took the packet of Brekkfast Brikks. At least it wasn't very big... On the front of the box was a picture of a fat, repulsive, fair-haired boy, rather like the chubby Augustus, banging on his plate with his spoon.

"They look like tiny doormats," said Mrs Armitage, as Mark shovelled some Brikks into his bowl.

"They taste like them too. Gosh," said Mark, "I must

hurry or I'll be late for school. There's rather a nice little cut-out garden on the back of the packet, though; don't throw it away when it's empty. Goodbye, Daddy," he shouted through the larder door. "Hope Mr Ellis comes soon to let you out." And he dashed off to catch the school bus.

At breakfast next morning Mark had a huge helping of Brekkfast Brikks and persuaded his father to try them.

"They taste just like esparto grass," said Mr Armitage fretfully.

"Yes I know, but do take some more, Daddy. I want to cut out the model garden, it's so lovely."

"Rather pleasant, I must say. It looks like an eighteenth-century German engraving," his father agreed. "It certainly was a stroke of genius putting it on the packet. No one would ever buy these things to eat for pleasure. Pass me the sugar, please. And the cream. And the strawberries."

It was half-term, so after breakfast Mark was able to take the empty packet away to the playroom and get on with the job of cutting out the stone walls, the row of little trees, the fountain, the yew-arch, the two green lawns, and the tiny clumps of brilliant flowers. He knew better than to 'stick tabs in slots and secure with paste' as the directions suggested; he had made models off packets before and knew they always fell to pieces unless they were firmly bound together with transparent sticky tape.

It was a long, fiddling, pleasurable job.

Nobody interrupted him. Mrs Armitage only cleared

the playroom once every six months or so, when she made a ferocious descent on it and tidied up the tape-recorders, roller-skates, meteorological sets, and dismantled railway-engines, and threw away countless old magazines, stringless tennis rackets, abandoned paintings, and unsuccessful models. There were always bitter complaints from Mark and Harriet; then they forgot and things piled up again till next time.

As Mark worked his eye was caught by a verse on the side of the packet:

> Brekkfast Brikks to start the day
> Make you fit in every way.
> Children bang their plates with glee
> At Brekkfast Brikks for lunch and tea!
> Brekkfast Brikks for supper too
> Give peaceful sleep the whole night through.

"Blimey," thought Mark, sticking a cedar tree into the middle of the lawn and then bending a stone wall round at dotted lines A, B, C and D. "I wouldn't want anything for breakfast, lunch, tea and supper, not even Christmas pudding. Certainly not Brekkfast Brikks."

He propped a clump of gaudy scarlet flowers against the wall and stuck them in place.

The words of the rhyme kept coming into his head as he worked and presently he found that they went rather well to a tune that was running through his mind, and he began to hum, and then to sing; Mark often did this when he was alone and busy.

> *"Brekkfast Brikks to sta-art the day,*
> *Ma-ake you fi-it in every way –*

"Blow, where did I put that little bit of sticky tape? Oh, there it is.

> *"Children bang their pla-ates with glee*
> *At Brekkfast Brikks for lunch and tea.*

"Slit gate with razor-blade, it says, but it'll have to be a penknife.

> *"Brekkfast Brikks for supper toohoo*
> *Give peaceful sleep the whole night throughoo...*

"Hullo. That's funny," said Mark.

It was funny. The openwork iron gate he had just stuck in position now suddenly towered above him. On either side, to right and left ran the high stone wall, stretching away into foggy distance. Over the top of the wall he could see tall trees, yews and cypresses and others he didn't know.

"Well, that's the neatest trick I ever saw," said Mark. "I wonder if the gate will open?"

He chuckled as he tried it, thinking of the larder door. The gate did open, and he went through into the garden.

One of the things that had already struck him as he cut them out was that the flowers were not at all in the right proportions. But they were all the nicer for that. There were huge velvety violets and pansies the size of saucers; the hollyhocks were as big as dinner-plates and the turf was sprinkled with enormous daisies. The roses, on the other hand, were miniature, no bigger than cuff-buttons. There were real fish in the fountain, bright pink.

"*I* made all this," thought Mark, strolling along the mossy path to the yew-arch. "Won't Harriet be surprised when she sees it. I wish she could see it now. I wonder what made it come alive like that?"

He passed through the yew-arch as he said this and discovered that on the other side there was nothing but grey, foggy blankness. This, of course, was where his cardboard garden ended. He turned back through the archway and gazed with pride at a border of huge scarlet tropical flowers which were perhaps supposed to be geraniums but certainly hadn't turned out that way. "I know! Of course it was the rhyme, the rhyme on the packet."

He recited it. Nothing happened. "Perhaps you have to sing it," he thought and (feeling a little foolish) he sang it through to the tune that fitted so well. At once, faster than blowing out a match, the garden drew itself together and shrank into its cardboard again, leaving Mark outside.

"What a marvellous hiding-place it'll make when I don't want people to come bothering," he thought. He sang the spell once more, just to make sure that it worked, and there was the high mossy wall, the stately iron gate, and the treetops. He stepped in and looked back. No playroom to be seen, only grey blankness.

At that moment he was startled by a tremendous clanging, the sort of sound the Trump of Doom would make if it were a dinner-bell. "Blow," he thought, "I suppose that's lunch." He sang the spell for the fourth time; immediately he was in the playroom, and the garden was on the table, and Agnes was still ringing the dinner-bell outside the door.

"All right, I heard," he shouted. "Just coming."

He glanced hurriedly over the remains of the packet to see if it bore any mention of the fact that the cut-out garden had magic properties. It did not. He did, however, learn that this was Section Three of the Beautiful Brekkfast Brikks Garden Series, and that Sections One, Two, Four, Five and Six would be found on other packets. In case of difficulty in obtaining supplies, please write to Frühstücksgeschirrziegelsteinindustrie (Great Britain), Lily Road, Shepherd's Bush.

"Elevenpence a packet," Mark murmured to himself, going to lunch with unwashed hands. "Five elevens are thirty-five. Thirty-five pennies are – no, that's wrong. Fifty-five pence are four and sevenpence. Father, if I mow the lawn and carry coal every day for a month, can I have four shillings and sevenpence?"

"You don't want to buy another space-gun, do you?"

said Mr Armitage looking at him suspiciously. "Because one is quite enough in this family."

"No, it's not for a space-gun, I swear."

"Oh, very well."

"And can I have the four and seven now?"

Mr Armitage gave it reluctantly. "But that lawn has to be like velvet, mind," he said. "And if there's any falling-off in the coal supply I shall demand my money back."

"No, no, there won't be," Mark promised earnestly. As soon as lunch was over he dashed down to Miss Pride's. Was there a chance that she would have Sections One, Two, Four, Five and Six? He felt certain that no other shop had even heard of Brekkfast Brikks, so she was his only hope, apart from the address in Shepherd's Bush.

"Oh, I don't know, I'm sure," Miss Pride said, sounding very doubtful – and more than a little surprised. "There might just be a couple on the bottom shelf – yes, here we are."

They were Sections Four and Five, bent and dusty, but intact, Mark saw with relief. "Don't you suppose you have any more anywhere?" he pleaded.

"I'll look in the cellar but I can't promise. I haven't had deliveries of any of these for a long time. Made by some foreign firm they were; people didn't seem very keen on them," Miss Pride said aggrievedly. She opened a door revealing a flight of damp stone stairs. Mark followed her down them like a bloodhound on the trail.

The cellar was a fearful confusion of mildewed, tattered and toppling cartons, some full, some empty. Mark was nearly knocked cold by a shower of pilchards in tins which he dislodged on to himself from the top of a heap of boxes. At last Miss Pride with a cry of triumph unearthed a little cache of Brekkfast Brikks, three packets, which turned out to be the remaining Sections, Six, One and Two.

"There, isn't that a piece of luck now!" she said, looking quite faint with all the excitement. It was indeed rare for Miss Pride to sell as many as five packets of the same thing at one time.

Mark galloped home with his booty and met his father in the porch. Mr Armitage let out a groan of dismay.

"I'd almost rather you'd bought a space-gun," he said.

"Brekkfast Brikks for supper too
Give peaceful sleep the whole night through.

"I don't want peaceful sleep," Mr Armitage said. "I intend to spend tonight mouse-watching again. I'm tired of finding footprints in the Stilton."

During the next few days Mark's parents watched anxiously to see, as Mr Armitage said, whether Mark would start to sprout esparto grass instead of hair. For he doggedly ate Brekkfast Brikks for lunch, with soup, or sprinkled over his pudding, for tea, with jam, and for supper lightly fried in dripping, not to mention, of course, the immense helpings he had for breakfast with sugar and milk. Mr Armitage for his part soon gave up; he said he wouldn't taste another Brekkfast Brikk even if it were wrapped in an inch-thick layer of *pâté-de-foie*. Mark regretted Harriet, who was a handy and uncritical eater, but she was still away convalescing from her measles with an aunt.

In two days the second packet was finished (sundial, paved garden, and espaliers). Mark cut it out, fastened it together, and joined it on to Section Three with trembling hands. Would the spell work for this section too? He sang the rhyme in rather a quavering voice, but luckily the playroom door was shut and there was no one to hear him. Yes! The gate grew again above him, and when he opened it and ran across the lawn through the yew-arch he found himself in a flagged garden full of flowers like huge blue cabbages.

Mark stood hugging himself with satisfaction, and then began to wander about smelling the flowers, which had a spicy perfume most unlike any flower he could think of. Suddenly he pricked up his ears. Had he caught a sound? There! It was like somebody crying, and seemed to come from the other side of the hedge. He ran to the next opening and looked through. Nothing: only grey mist and emptiness. But, unless he had imagined it, just before he got there he thought his eye had caught the flash of white and gold draperies swirling past the gateway.

"Do you think Mark's all right?" Mrs Armitage said to her husband next day. "He seems to be in such a dream all the time."

"Boy's gone clean off his rocker if you ask me," grumbled Mr Armitage. "It's all these doormats he's eating. Can't be good to stuff your insides with mouldy jute. Still I'm bound to say he's cut the lawn very decently and seems to be remembering the coal. I'd better take a day off from the office and drive you over to the shore for a picnic; sea air will do him good."

Mrs Armitage suggested to Mark that he should slack off on the Brekkfast Brikks, but he was so horrified that she had to abandon the idea. But, she said, he was to run four times round the garden every morning before breakfast. Mark almost said "Which garden?" and stopped just in time. He had cut out and completed another large lawn, with a lake and weeping willows, and on the far side of the lake had a tantalizing glimpse of a figure dressed in white and gold who moved away and was lost before he could get there.

After munching his way through the fourth packet he was able to add on a broad grass walk bordered by curiously clipped trees. At the end of the walk he could see the white and gold person, but when he ran to the spot no one was there – the walk ended in the usual grey mist.

When he had finished and cut out the fifth packet (an orchard) a terrible thing happened to him. For two days he could not remember the tune that worked the spell. He tried other tunes, but they were no use. He sat in the playroom singing till he was hoarse, or silent with despair. Suppose he never remembered it again?

His mother shook her head at him that evening and said he looked as if he needed a dose. "It's lucky we're going to Shinglemud Bay for the day tomorrow," she said. "That ought to do you good."

"Oh, *blow*. I'd forgotten about that," Mark said. "Need I go?"

His mother stared at him in utter astonishment.

But in the middle of the night he remembered the right tune, leapt out of bed in a tremendous hurry, and ran down to the playroom without even waiting to put on his dressing-gown and slippers.

The orchard was most wonderful, for instead of mere apples its trees bore oranges, lemons, limes, and all sorts of tropical fruits whose names he did not know, and there were melons and pineapples growing, and plantains and avocados. Better still, he saw the lady in her white and gold waiting at the end of an alley and was able to draw near enough to speak.

"Who are you?" she asked. She seemed very astonished at the sight of him.

"My name is Mark Armitage," he said politely. "Is this your garden?"

Close to, he saw that she was really very grand indeed. Her dress was white satin embroidered with pearls, and swept the ground; she had a gold scarf and her hair, dressed high and powdered, was confined in a small gold-and-pearl tiara. Her face was rather plain, pink with a long nose, but she had a kind expression and beautiful grey eyes.

"Indeed it is," she announced with hauteur. "I am Princess Sophia Maria Louisa of Saxe-Hoffenpoffen-und-Hamster. What are you doing here, pray?"

"Well," Mark explained cautiously, "it seemed to come about through singing a tune."

"Indeed? That is most interesting. Did the tune, perhaps, go like this?" This princess hummed a few bars.

"That's it! How did you know?"

"Why, you foolish boy, it was I who put the spell on the garden, to make it come alive when the tune is played or sung."

"I say!" Mark was full of admiration. "Can you do magic as well as being a princess?"

She drew herself up. "Naturally! At the court of Saxe-Hoffenpoffen where I was educated all princesses were taught a little magic – not so much as to be vulgar, just enough to get out of social difficulties."

"Jolly useful," Mark said. "How did you work the spell for the garden, then?"

"Why, you see," (the princess was obviously delighted to have somebody to talk to; she sat on a stone seat and patted it, inviting Mark to do likewise.) "I had the misfortune to fall in love with Herr Rudolf, the Court Kapellmeister, who taught me music. Oh, he was so kind and handsome! And he was most talented, but my father, of course, would not hear of my marrying him because he was only a common person."

"So what did you do?"

"I arranged to vanish, of course. Rudi had given me a beautiful book with many pictures of gardens. My father kept strict watch to see I did not run away, so I slipped between the pages of the book, having first asked my maid to take it to Rudi that evening. And I posted him a note telling him to play the tune when he received the book. But I believe that spiteful Gertrud must have played me false and never taken the book, for more than fifty years have now passed and I have been here all alone, waiting in the garden, and Rudi has never come. Oh, Rudi, Rudi," she exclaimed, wringing her hands and crying a little, "where can you be? It is so long – so long!"

"Fifty years," Mark said kindly, reckoning that must make her nearly seventy. "I must say you don't look it."

"Of course I do not, dumbhead. For me, I make it that time does not touch me. But tell me, how did you know the tune that works the spell? It was taught me by my dear Rudi."

"I'm not sure where I picked it up," Mark confessed. "For all I know it may be one of the Top Ten. I'll ask my music teacher, he's sure to know. Perhaps he'll have heard of your Rudolf too."

Privately Mark feared that Rudolf might very well have died by now, but he did not like to depress Princess Sophia Maria by such a suggestion, so he bade her a polite good night, promising to come back as soon as he could with another section of garden and any news he could pick up.

He planned to go and see Mr Johansen, his music teacher, next morning, but he had forgotten the family trip to the beach. There was just time to scribble a hasty postcard to the British office of Frühstücksgeschirrziegelsteinindustrie, asking them if they could inform him from what source they had obtained the pictures used on the packets of Brekkfast Brikks. Then Mr Armitage drove his wife and son to Shinglemud Bay, gloomily prophesying wet weather.

In fact the weather turned out fine, and Mark found it quite restful to swim and play beach cricket and eat ham sandwiches and lie in the sun. For he had been struck by a horrid thought: suppose he should forget the tune again when he was inside the garden – would he be stuck there, like Father in the larder? It was a lovely place to go and wander at will, but somehow he didn't fancy spending the next fifty years there with Princess Sophia Maria. Would she oblige him by singing the spell if he forgot it, or would she be too keen on company to let him go? He was not inclined to take any chances.

It was late when they arrived home, too late, Mark thought, to disturb Mr Johansen, who was elderly and kept early hours. Mark ate a huge helping of sardines on Brekkfast Brikks for supper – he was dying to finish Section Six – but did not visit the garden that night.

Next morning's breakfast (Brikks with hot milk for a change) finished the last packet – and just as well, for the larder mouse, which Mr Armitage still had not caught, was discovered to have nibbled the bottom left-hand corner of the packet, slightly damaging an ornamental grotto in a grove of lime-trees. Rather worried about this, Mark decided to make up the last section straight away, in case the magic had been affected. By now he was becoming very skilful at the tiny fiddling task of cutting out the little tabs and slipping them into the little slots; the job did not take long to finish. Mark attached Section Six to Section Five and then, drawing a deep breath, sang the incantation once more. With immense relief he watched the mossy wall and rusty gate grow out of the playroom floor; all was well.

He raced across the lawn, round the lake, along the avenue, through the orchard, and into the lime-grove. The scent of the lime-flowers was sweeter than a cake baking.

Princess Sophia Maria came towards him from the grotto, looking slightly put out.

"Good morning!" she greeted Mark. "Do you bring me any news?"

"I haven't been to see my music teacher yet," Mark confessed. "I was a bit anxious because there was a hole—"

"Ach, yes, a hole in the grotto! I have just been looking. Some wild beast must have made its way in, and I am afraid it may come again. See, it has made tracks like those of a big bear." She showed him some enormous footprints in the soft sand of the grotto floor. Mark stopped up the hole with prickly branches and promised to bring a dog when he next came, though he felt fairly sure the mouse would not return.

"I can borrow a dog from my teacher – he has plenty. I'll be back in an hour or so – see you then," he said.

"*Auf wiedersehen*, my dear young friend."

Mark ran along the village street to Mr Johansen's house, Houndshaven Cottage. He knew better than to knock at the door because Mr Johansen would be either practising his violin or out in the barn at the back, and in any case the sound of barking was generally loud enough to drown any noise short of gun-fire.

Besides giving music lessons at Mark's school, Mr Johansen kept a guest-house for dogs whose owners were abroad or on holiday. He was extremely kind to the guests and did his best to make them feel at home in every way, finding out from their owners what were their favourite foods, and letting them sleep on his own bed, turn about. He spent all his spare time with them, talking to them and playing either his violin or LP records of domestic sounds likely to appeal to the canine fancy – such as knives being sharpened, cars starting up, and children playing ball-games.

Mark could hear Mr Johansen playing Brahms's Lullaby in the barn, so he went out there; the music was making some of the more susceptible inmates feel homesick: howls, sympathetic moans, and long shuddering sighs came from the numerous comfortably carpeted cubicles all the way down the barn.

Mr Johansen reached the end of the piece as Mark entered. He put down his fiddle and smiled welcomingly.

"Ach, how *gut*! It is the young Mark."

"Hullo, sir."

"You know," confided Mr Johansen, "I play to many audiences in my life all over the world, but never anywhere do I get such a response as from zese dear doggies – it is really remarkable. But come in, come in to ze house and have some coffee-cake."

Mr Johansen was a gentle, white-haired elderly man; he walked slowly with a slight stoop and had a kindly sad face with large dark eyes; he looked rather like some sort of dog himself, Mark always thought, perhaps a collie or a long-haired dachshund.

"Sir," Mark said, "if I whistle a tune to you, can you write it down for me?"

"Why yes, I shall be most happy," Mr Johansen said, pouring coffee for both of them.

So Mark whistled his tune once more; as he came to the end he was surprised to see the music master's eyes fill with tears, which slowly began to trickle down his thin cheeks.

"It recalls my youth, zat piece," he explained, wiping them away and rapidly scribbling crochets and minims on a piece of music paper. "Many times I am whistling it myself — it is wissout doubt from me you learn it — but always it is reminding me of how happy I was long ago when I wrote it."

"You *wrote* that tune?" Mark said, much excited.

"Why yes. What is so strange in zat? Many, many tunes haf I written."

"Well," Mark said, "I won't tell you just yet in case I'm mistaken — I'll have to see somebody else first. Do you mind if I dash off right away? Oh, and might I borrow a dog — preferably a good ratter?"

"In zat case, better have my dear Lotta — alzough she is so old she is ze best of zem all," Mr Johansen said proudly. Lotta was his own dog, an enormous shaggy lumbering animal with a tail like a palm-tree and feet the size of electric polishers; she was reputed to be of incalculable age; Mr Johansen called her his strudel-hound. She knew Mark well and came along with him quite biddably, though it was rather like leading a mammoth.

Luckily his mother, refreshed by her day at the sea, was heavily engaged with Agnes the maid in spring-cleaning. Furniture was being shoved about and everyone was too busy to notice Mark and Lotta slip into the playroom.

A letter addressed to Mark lay among the clutter on the table; he opened and read it while Lotta foraged happily among the piles of magazines and tennis nets and cricket bats and rusting electronic equipment, managing to upset several things and increase the general state of hugger-mugger in the room.

The letter was from Messrs Digit, Digit & Rule, a firm of chartered accountants, and said:

Dear Sir,

We are in receipt of your inquiry as to the source of pictures on packets of Brekkfast Brikks. We are pleased to inform you that these were reproduced from the illustrations of a little-known eighteenth-century German work, Steinbergen's *Gartenbuch*. Unfortunately the only known remaining copy of this book was burnt in the disastrous fire which destroyed the factory and premises of Messrs Frühstücksgeschirrziegelsteinindustrie two months ago. The firm has now gone into liquidation and we are winding up their effects.

Yours faithfully,

P. J. ZERO, Gen. Sec.

"Steinbergen's *Gartenbuch*," Mark thought. "That must have been the book that Princess Sophia used for the spell – probably the same copy. Oh well, since it's burnt, it's lucky the pictures were reproduced on the Brekkfast Brikk packs. Come on, Lotta, let's go and find a nice princess then. Good girl! Rats! Chase 'em!"

He sang the spell and Lotta, all enthusiasm, followed him into the garden.

They did not have to go far before they saw the princess – she was sitting sunning herself on the rim of the fountain. But what happened then was unexpected. Lotta let out the most extraordinary cry – whine, bark and howl all in one – and hurled herself towards the princess like a rocket.

"Hey! Look out! Lotta! *Heel!*" Mark shouted in alarm. But Lotta, with her great paws on the princess's shoulders, had about a yard of salmon-pink tongue out, and was washing her face all over with frantic affection.

The princess was just as excited. "Lotta! Lotta! She knows me, it's dear Lotta, it must be! Where did you get her?" she cried to Mark, hugging the enormous dog whose tail was going round faster than a turbo-prop.

"Why, she belongs to my music master, Mr Johansen, and it's he who made up the tune," Mark said.

The princess turned quite white, and had to sit down on the fountain's rim again.

"*Johansen?* Rudolf Johansen? My Rudi! At last! After all these years! Oh, run, run, and fetch him immediately, please! Immediately!"

Mark hesitated a moment.

"Please make haste!" she besought him. "Why do you wait?"

"It's only – well, you won't be surprised if he's quite *old*, will you? Remember he hasn't been in a garden keeping young like you."

"All that will change," the princess said confidently. "He has only to eat the fruit of the garden. Why, look at Lotta – when she was a puppy, for a joke I gave her a fig from this tree, and you can see she is a puppy still, though she must be older than any other dog in the world! Oh, please hurry to bring Rudi here."

"Why don't you come with me to his house?"

"That would not be correct etiquette," she said with dignity. "After all, I *am* royal."

"Okay," said Mark. I'll fetch him. Hope he doesn't think I'm crackers."

"Give him this." The princess took off a locket on a gold chain. It had a miniature of a romantically handsome young man with dark curling hair. "My Rudi," she explained fondly. Mark could just trace a faint resemblance to Mr Johansen.

He took the locket and hurried away. At the gate

something made him look back: the princess and Lotta were sitting at the edge of the fountain, side by side. The princess had an arm round Lotta's neck; with the other hand she waved to him, just a little.

"Hurry!" she called again.

Mark made his way out of the house, through the spring-cleaning chaos, and flew down the village to Houndshaven Cottage. Mr Johansen was in the house this time, boiling up a noisome mass of meat and bones for the dogs' dinner. Mark said nothing at all, just handed him the locket. He took one look at it and staggered, putting his hand to his heart; anxiously, Mark led him to a chair.

"Are you all right, sir?"

"Yes, yes! It was only ze shock. Where did you get ziss, my boy?"

So Mark told him.

Surprisingly, Mr Johansen did not find anything odd about the story; he nodded his head several times as Mark related the various points.

"Yes, yes, her letter, I have it still — " he pulled out a worn little scrap of paper — "but ze *Gartenbuch* it reached me never. Zat wicked Gertrud must haf sold it to some bookseller who sold it to Frühstücksgeschirrziegelsteinindustrie. And so she has been waiting all ziss time! My poor little Sophie!"

"Are you strong enough to come to her now?" Mark asked.

"*Natürlich!* But first we must give ze dogs zeir dinner; zey must not go hungry."

So they fed the dogs, which was a long job, as there were at least sixty, and each had a different diet, including some very odd preferences like Swiss Roll spread with Marmite, and yeast pills wrapped in slices of caramel. Privately, Mark thought the dogs were a bit spoilt, but Mr Johansen was very careful to see that each visitor had just what it fancied.

"After all, zey are not mine! Must I not take good care of zem?"

At least two hours had gone by before the last willow-pattern plate was licked clean and they were free to go. Mark made rings round Mr Johansen all the way up the village; the music master limped quietly along, smiling a little; from time to time he said, "Gently, my friend. We do not run a race. Remember I am an old man."

This was just what Mark did remember. He longed to see Mr Johansen young and happy once more.

The chaos in the Armitage house had changed its location: the front hall was now clean, tidy and damp; the rumpus of vacuuming had shifted to the playroom. With a black hollow of apprehension in his middle, Mark ran through the open door, and stopped, aghast. All the toys, tools, weapons, boxes, magazines and bits of machinery had been rammed into the cupboards; the table where his garden had been laid out was bare. Mrs Armitage was in there taking down the curtains.

"*Mother!* Where's my Brekkfast Brikks garden?"

"Oh, darling, you didn't want it, did you? It was all

dusty, I thought you'd finished with it. I'm afraid I've burnt it in the furnace. Really you *must* try not to let this room get into such a clutter, it's perfectly disgraceful. – Why, hullo, Mr Johansen," she added in embarrassment, "I didn't see you, I'm afraid you've called at the worst possible moment. But I'm sure you'll understand how it is at spring-cleaning time."

She rolled up her bundle of curtains, glancing worriedly at Mr Johansen; he looked rather odd, she thought. But he gave her his tired, gentle smile, and said:

"Why, yes, Mrs Armitage, I understand, I understand very well. Come, Mark. We have no business here, you can see."

Speechlessly, Mark followed him. What was there to say?

"Never mind," Mrs Armitage called after Mark. "The Rice Nuts packet has a helicopter on it."

Every week in *The Times* newspaper you will see this advertisement:

"BREKKFAST BRIKKS PACKETS. £100 offered for any in good condition, whether empty or full."

So if you have any, you know where to send them.

Postscript

People sometimes ask me, which do you enjoy more, writing for children or writing for adults? And my usual reply is, when I am doing one, I am looking forward to the other kind of writing.

It is not so much a matter of plot, or characters, or language; the more books I write, the more these frontiers seem to melt away, and to matter less and less. Perhaps young readers are growing more adult in their tastes. Or perhaps their parents, who grew up on C. S. Lewis and Tolkien, are harking back more to the kind of reading they enjoyed in their teens. I get letters, sometimes, from families who say they all enjoy my books together. Which makes me very happy, because some of the best memories of my childhood are connected with the way we all used to read aloud to each other, the things that we ourselves enjoyed; my elder brother used to read Damon Runyan's *Guys and Dolls* stories, or the short stories of Saki; my elder sister used to read historical novels, *The Count of Monte Cristo* or *The Chaplet of Pearls*; my mother used to read Dickens, or the Bible, or Milton, or Masefield; my stepfather used to read Russian authors, Tolstoy or Dostoevsky; and we all used to read to my younger brother, Ransome books or *The Hobbit* or a book he liked better than anything else in the world, *Mumfie's Magic Box*, which must have been read aloud to him at least three hundred and nineteen times.

During World War Two my mother used to run a kind of unofficial lending library for London children who were evacuated to our village to escape the bombing. And a lot of our books got borrowed and never returned, but I have replaced them from second-hand bookshops as years went by. One that I mourned very much was a fantasy novel by the poet Walter de la Mare called *The Three Mulla-Mulgars*. It was a strange, romantic tale about three monkey brothers who set off to look for their lost father through a world of everlasting winter and all kinds of perils; it had wonderful pictures by an American illustrator called Dorothy Lathrop. When I was asked by the American Library Association to mention which book I loved most and had the most influence on me in my childhood, I named this book and said how much I missed it. Not long afterwards a country library in America sent me a copy of the book which had been donated from the belongings of a customer who had died – it was the same edition, with the same pictures, and the pages were still uncut!

Anyway, as I said above, when I am asked which kind of writing I prefer, I tend to say that it is the kind I am *not* doing at the moment. For a book takes quite a long time to write. I generally reckon that a novel, whether for children or adults, takes nine months to plan, and nine months to write. (While I am doing that planning and writing, I am thinking about the next one; and making notes, and stuffing them into a folder.) And before starting to write, I make a plan, with squares for chapters, and notes about what is going to happen in each chapter, and, if possible, the last line of the last chapter written in, like a target, or the light at the end of the tunnel. So a novel is quite a serious undertaking, whether for adults or children.

But short stories are something completely different. They arrive at all kinds of odd times, and have nothing to do with the weighty business of writing novels. Stories are like butterflies, which come fluttering out of nowhere, touch down for a brief instant, may be captured – may not – and then vanish into nowhere again.

So the truthful answer to the question, "Do you prefer writing for adults or children?" would be, "I prefer writing short stories." They come from nowhere, and they are aimed at nobody's ear; or rather, they are aimed at the ear of anybody who happens to pass by just at that moment. A story called *The Three Travellers* came into my head one evening as I was walking across Wimbledon Common. It went into a children's collection, but it might just as well have been aimed at adults. A story called *The People in the Castle* came into my mind when I lived in the town of Lewes, in Sussex, and was waiting to see my doctor, whose surgery and waiting room, in those days, were in Lewes Castle.

A Small Pinch of Weather was also set in Lewes, but not written until ten years after I had left that town and was travelling up to London every day on a train from Haslemere to Waterloo. There were two shops side by side between the car park where I left my car and Haslemere station; one of them was called WOOLS AND EMBROIDERY and the other one was called JOY. I never discovered what it sold. From across the road the two signs read together as WOOLS AND JOY. From that juxtaposition came the idea of Wools and Weather and a shopkeeper who sold knitting wool or an April shower alternately to her customers. When I lived in Lewes I was next-door to a guesthouse where a Bishop used to come and stay regularly, and our cat had the wayward habit of going over the roof and dropping in on the Bishop through his skylight, so half the story was there already. Sometimes stories arrive in that way; half has been waiting, unfertilised, in one's unconscious mind, sometimes for years, until the second element arrives and triggers it off.

Short stories are wonderful fun to write, really exhilarating; they are like being taken for a quick ride on a magic carpet. I can remember various moments when the explosive idea for a story first hit me: peeling potatoes when I was running a guesthouse and talking to Nicky, the teenage son of one of the guests; or the actual occasion, on a Saturday when I happened to be alone in my stepfather's cottage and a lady in an expensive motor stopped, ran up the steps, rang the bell, and wanted to buy his quince tree, which hung over the road, because she ran a well-known gardening programme and had pretended she had a quince tree and now needed one in a hurry; or the dream that landed me with a story called *Hope*, a sad, sinister dream about an old lady who taught the harp, meeting the Devil and his pop group in a nest of alleyways somewhere in that shady part of London that I call Rumbury Town; or the story called *Smoke from Cromwell's Time* that came to me all in a flash just in time to fill a gap in a collection if I wrote it at once and, because there was a postal strike, sent it to London by my brother who was driving up that night...

The collection was called *A Small Pinch of Weather*. I have written about twenty-seven collections of short stories so far, but some of the stories in this batch I still think are among my very best work, and I am happy that they are going to be in print again.

Favourite stories, like unexpected presents, are things that you can keep and cherish all your life, carry with you, in memory, in your mind's ear, and bring out, at any time, when you are feeling lonely, or need cheering up, or, like friends, just because you are fond of them. That is the way I feel about some of the stories in this collection – stories, for instance, like *The Serial Garden*. One day I will write a sequel to that story, but not just yet...

JOAN AIKEN
March 2000